THE

OLD

REACTOR

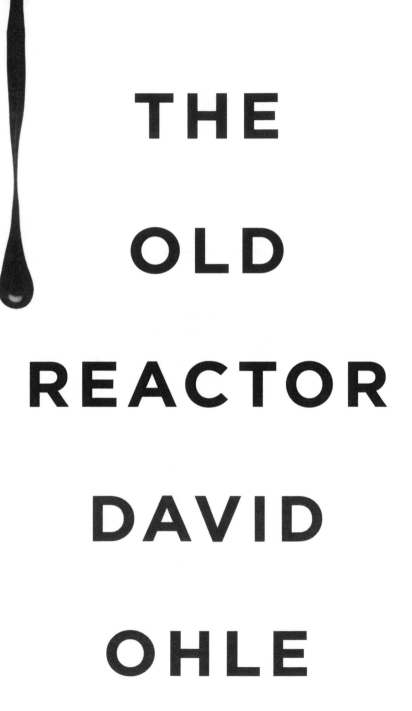

THE

OLD

REACTOR

DAVID

OHLE

DZANC
BOOKS

DZANC BOOKS

5220 Dexter Ann Arbor Rd.
Ann Arbor, MI 48103
www.dzancbooks.org

Designed by Steven Seighman

Library of Congress Cataloging-in-Publication Data

Ohle, David.
   The old reactor : a novel / by David Ohle.
      pages cm
   I. Title.

PS3565.H6O53 2014
813'.54—dc23

                                        2014013419

ISBN: 978-1936873562

First U.S. Edition: September 2014

Printed in the United States of America

10   9   8   7   6   5   4   3   2   1

When we have communicated nicely within ourselves, the stool reflects a simple reasonable operation (cowflop is, for example, modest in its odor) but where we have failed...the odors and shapes are tortured, corrupt, rich, fascinating (that is attractive and repulsive at the same time) theatrical, even tragic."

—Norman Mailer, "The Metaphysics of the Belly"

THE

OLD

REACTOR

In those days Moldenke stayed in the city of Bunkerville and was so full of passion for the labor movement his nose bled when he spoke of it. He could be seen day after day going up and down Esplanade Avenue in the company of a few like-minded friends, passing out the pamphlet, "Fair Play for the Working Stiff." He knew, though, that his bowel could make sudden demands. Wherever he picketed or passed out leaflets, the location of the nearest public toilet was always something to keep in mind. The condition had come upon him in his teens, in school at St. Cuthbert's. Doctors told him it was a stubborn inflammation that could last the rest of his life. They had given it a name he had long ago forgotten.

It was also a time when his dear aunt lay dying of a persistent and growing abdominal teratoma. She lay tucked into a narrow room at the Broad Street Charnel House, living out her last days. It was an awful place and Moldenke hated going there, yet he did so religiously every Sunday.

His aunt's surgeon, the well-known scientist Edgar Zanzetti, could do no more. It was now up to her to settle into dying. The growth that protruded from her abdomen looked to Moldenke like an apple under a tablecloth. Weakened muscles in her drooping lids required that she wear small lid-lifting appliances made of gold plated rods and rubber knobs. She was a plaster mold of her former self who'd come to look like an illustration in a medical text.

When he went to see her on those anxious Sunday afternoons, Moldenke's stomach burned and his hands shook. He'd been living in her house on Esplanade for nine months, keeping an eye on things while she underwent surgery after surgery. He paid no rent, nor had he done well keeping an eye on things. The house had been broken into many times. Antique silver services, jewelry, rare first editions, musical instruments, and a beaver coat had been stolen.. The thieves came in almost nightly while Moldenke slept upstairs with cotton in his ears to shut out the noise of the streetcars running on Esplanade.

He paid no particular interest to maintenance or sanitation. The rusting gutters sagged with a load of leaves and twigs. Windows had been left open during rain storms, leaving soaked carpets in the parlor and buckled tiles in the kitchen. Rarely had the dishes been washed, the vacuum cleaner had never been taken from its closet under the stairs, there were generations of wharf rats living under the kitchen sink, and a frilly gray fungus thrived on curtains and walls.

As soon as Moldenke arrived at the Charnel that Sunday, his aunt began to needle him, a froth forming at the corner of her lips. "How many times did your mother read you the fable of the grasshopper and the ant?"

"Not that again."

The little nook where she was kept was so narrow that Moldenke could not stand at the side of her cot but had to remain in the doorway a few feet away. He lit a cork-tipped Julep, inhaled, then let the smoke out as he said, "You conveniently forget the tortoise and the hare. She read that, too. I'm off to a slow start, but I could have a strong finish. That's the lesson I took."

"Please don't smoke those things in here. They smell like burning hair."

"All right." He smashed the Julep out on the bottom of his shoe and slid the leftover stub into his shirt pocket for later.

"Worse times are ahead," his aunt warned. "You know that, don't you? They liberated Altobello. Bunkerville will be next."

"I'm as ready as anyone," he said. "For anything."

"Have you found work? Idle hands are the devil's workshop. You know that."

"My friends and I will be picketing Eternity Meadows later. I don't have time to look for a job today. Do you have any idea what they pay their grave diggers?"

"You'll get into trouble. They'll send you to Altobello on a freighter."

"It hardly matters. I wouldn't mind going there. Some pure freedom might be good for a while. Scary, but interesting."

"What about the jellyheads? They've been infesting the place. It's been in the papers."

Moldenke had seen jellies walking the streets of Bunkerville, too, but didn't want to frighten his aunt with the real news. Instead, he opened a waxed paper envelope. "I brought you a bear claw. You love them."

"I'm too sick to eat. You bring them for yourself."

"Yes, I know." He ate a bite of the sugary confection, rolling balls of it on his tongue before swallowing.

"Still taking care of my house on Esplanade, or have you found a place of your own?"

"If I weren't living there, who would? The house is a shambles. You couldn't rent it to jellyheads. I'm doing you a favor by staying in it."

His aunt made a strenuous but successful effort to turn onto her side and say, "You'll find a nice pretty girl someday. You can live with her in my house."

"Thank you, Aunt."

With another thrust she attempted to turn onto her back. Moldenke made a move toward helping but could reach only her feet. If he hadn't been afraid of breaking her ankles he might have tried to twist them to help her roll. She managed to turn with an exhausting struggle. In the process, her lid lifters fell to the floor and her eyelids drooped. It took her a few minutes to catch her breath. "Can you get my lifters for me?"

The distance between the wall and the cot was only a few inches. Moldenke couldn't reach the lifters without climbing into the cot with his aunt. "I can't get to them. I'm sorry."

She pinched her nose. "You smell. That bowel of yours isn't getting any better, is it? You've shit your pants, haven't you?"

Moldenke looked upward, as if there were something eye-catching above him. "They haven't been washed for a while."

"Dear nephew, is the ceiling easier to look than I am?"

"That lump is just something I'd rather not see. Zanzetti told me those kinds of tumors have hair and teeth and small bones in them. And I don't want to talk about my angry bowel, either. I have to go."

"I may die tonight, or tomorrow, so there is something I've kept from you."

"Hurry, tell me again."

"When your father woke up that morning your mother was standing naked at the foot of the bed in a puddle of water and blood saying, 'He's here too soon!' Your father spread bath towels on the bedroom floor. The labor was short. A few contractions and there you were. You came to them the way the Sunday paper is thrown on the porch. They were expecting it, but were startled when it dropped."

"I've heard this a hundred times."

"Such a nice boy. Give you a few pins, a cigar box, a handful of mothballs, and there you'd go, collecting earwigs and spittle bugs and having the time of your life."

"I really have to leave. My friends and I are picketing."

"You made molds of your fingers with paraffin, filled them with plaster and lined the dresser top with these little monuments to yourself. You even tried to make a mold of your little Johnny Brown, but the hot paraffin burned you."

"How many times have I heard *that* one? I'm going."

"It was cute the way you couldn't make up your mind about anything."

"Please stop."

"The simplest questions, you never answered them.... What did you have for lunch at school? You'd hem, you'd haw, you'd look down at your shoes as if they were golden slippers."

"I overthink things sometimes, granted. I'm leaving. I really am."

"And let me say, I find it odd that you care so much for the worker, yet you don't work."

"My work is working for the worker."

"Without pay? The worker is doing better than you are. Don't you see it?"

"I have to go."

"I suppose I'm in general sympathy with your fair-wage cause, but I'm afraid it will all end badly. I can see in you and your friends the promise of fanaticism. I'm convinced nothing good can come of it all."

"Thank you for that strong encouragement."

"Look in my closet at home for a shoebox. There's about ten million in there to get me a decent burial. I want to be in Eternity Meadows."

"All right. I'll take care of that. But in case you're not dead by next Sunday, I'll visit again."

"When I'm gone, aside from the ten mill for my burial, you'll inherit my house on Esplanade and a sum of money in trust for the maintenance and repair. As for your personal maintenance, you'll have to find work, fair wage or not. Dig graves if you have to."

"I'll manage."

She pulled the sheet over her head. "Dig mine if you get the chance."

"There's the spirit. See you next Sunday."

After these visits, Moldenke hurried over to the Come On Inn, a tavern just across from City Park. A few glasses of strong bitters took away the shakes that seeing his aunt gave him. He'd always had a visceral aversion to the sick and dying and wanted no part of it. Dying should always be done alone, he thought, but all too often wasn't. He and the aunt were the only living Moldenkes. He had no choice but to look after her post mortems.

Jellyhead children with blue teeth were seen roaming aimlessly in City Park. Homeless and underfed, abandoned by frightened parents, they refused all food and drink left for them, preferring to eat grasshoppers and drink water from a drainage ditch. It is known that a type of jaundice related to an infection of the blood can cause bluing teeth and loss of appetite, but nothing can account for the other anomalies in their appearance and behavior. For one, they were hairless and as pale as chalk. For another, their ear valves were unusually well developed and their leg muscles were atrophied, giving them a stork-like gait. They beat one another mercilessly with sticks. The weakest among them were dragged to the park lagoon and drowned. Like goats, they relieve themselves wherever the urge strikes. Park visitors have been hit with slingshot stones and splattered with thrown stool.

A week later, when Moldenke visited his aunt again, she was barely conscious. He didn't think she would be around by the following Sunday. For the entire week, he devoted his time to more or less arranging her funeral and burial. When he arrived at Eternity Meadows, hoping to find an affordable gravesite near the back fence, some of his pro-labor friends were picketing outside the gate. Their banner read, "A Living Wage for the Living Worker." One of them, Ozzie, an old friend of Moldenke's, made no effort to conceal the small caliber pistol he carried in his belt.

A bystander warned anyone approaching, "Don't cross the line, he's been threatening to shoot people."

While Moldenke took the warning seriously, he felt sure his friend would make an exception in his case, which he did, but not without a great deal of bluster and display, even once drawing his pistol and waving it in Moldenke's face. "Are you with us or against us? You haven't been picketing."

"There's going to be a death in the family, an aunt, my last living relative. After her, I'm all alone in the world. She'll need a place to be buried. I can't be picketing anymore."

"All right, go on in. You can have an hour."

The cemetery was a pleasant, quiet place to be that afternoon, especially with Moldenke's pals keeping everyone out. Though the weather had turned cold there were still thick morning glory vines, dying now, that had weaved themselves through and around all the spaces in the chain-link fence. Moldenke recalled summer walks in the cemetery, dragon flies flitting from one tombstone to another and little green lizards atop a few of them showed their dewlaps. For a moment he felt utterly calm, collected, and at peace. But as he looked among the empty plots for one that seemed affordable, he was stricken by a terrible urgency in his abdomen. There would be no time to find a toilet, even if he ran back to his aunt's house or to a public privy, so he walked, skipped, and trotted as fast as he could to the tallest head stone he could see and squatted behind it to relieve himself.

When he was finished, he used the only thing handy to wipe: a bouquet of withered flowers from the nearest vase. Standing and belting his pants, he bowed his head, clasped his hands, and addressed an apology to the deceased. "I'm so sorry. I hope you'll forgive me for being such a dog. My bowel can't be controlled. Don't worry, the sun will come along and dry it out in a day or two and the wind will blow it away."

The picketers sat on the ground, handcuffed, bleeding from head and facial wounds as Moldenke was leaving the cemetary. One was being questioned by a police officer who had torn up the 'living wage' banner.

Moldenke made a sharp turn and hurried down Esplanade toward City Canal. But before he was across the silver-painted swing bridge, the officer yelled, "Hey! You! Stop!"

Moldenke waited until the officer made his way to the bridge.

"Yes, Officer?"

"Sir, one of the gravediggers says he saw you take a crap on someone's resting place. True?"

"Yes, but I do have a chronic condition with my bowels. Sudden attacks. Almost no warning."

"No matter how you sugar-coat it, that's desecrating a grave. You're probably going to Altobello."

"How could I be sent there for this? You're trying to fill a quota to populate the place. I really don't mind going, but I've got a dying aunt. I'll have to take care of her body when she goes. I need some time."

"Don't smart mouth me and don't make all those excuses." The officer cuffed Moldenke. "Shitting on a grave is not child's play."

"Who will bury my aunt if I'm sent to Altobello? Who'll arrange some kind of ceremony?"

The officer hiked up his shiny blue pants. "You've got a couple of weeks before you leave. You better hope she goes pretty quick."

It was reported in the *City Moon* that in the liberated city of Altobello, a jellyhead woman who lived near the Old Reactor entered Saposcat's Deli on Arden Boulevard last night with five severed heads in a suitcase, those of her husband, Barry; her twin ten-year-olds, Muffy and Dale; Earnest, the blind and deaf son; and George D. Bennett, an uncle visiting from Bunkerville.

Observers say she sat with a calm demeanor, though her clothes were blood soaked and glistening with gel and her suitcase oozing. She ordered a flash-fried mud fish plate from a trembling waitress. The fry cook prepared the order as quickly as he could. After eating a few bites of the salty fish and drinking a soda, the woman suddenly shouted, "Oh, shit! I forgot about little Timmy," then dashed from the restaurant.

Shortly, she returned with her youngest's head in a soaked and dripping cloth bag. Now her family was complete. She finished her meal and called for the waitress.

"I'm through, thanks. You can take my plate."

"Would you like dessert? We have sweetened kerd, we have—"

"No. I'm leaving these heads here and going. I have some ground to cover in a short time." She waved in a grand gesture to the entire restaurant, let out a squirt or two from her ear valves, slid from her booth, and left at a slow trot.

As the diners looked on, some in shock, some amused, the fry cook opened the woman's suitcase and the bag and said, "We've got six heads here. Personally speaking, I've never seen a jelly bring in more than three at once. Don't ask me why they sever them like that or why they always drop them off at Saposcat's. I don't have a clue. They don't seem to know what they're doing."

The beheadings of loved ones was something new to the native jellies of Altobello, who were formerly devoted to family, to the home, to community values, until they set up an encampment out near the Old Reactor about a hundred years ago and began drinking heavy water from the Reactor's storage vessels in the belief that it was an all-around tonic for general health. After that custom became a part of their culture, there was no predicting how a given jellyhead might behave. They sometimes went critical.

Moldenke looked over the obits every day in the *City Moon*, always a little displeased after reading down the list of hundreds of dead that his aunt's name wasn't there. He only had two weeks before he would have to make other arrangements, to find her a plot, to have a ceremony, to arrange at least a few words by someone in some kind of vestment. And the house on Esplanade—who would live there and watch the place while he was gone? And could they be trusted to spend his aunt's maintenance money wisely?

More pressing now was to find her a decent resting place without spending any more of the ten mill than necessary.

On days when his aunt's name wasn't in the paper, Moldenke wasted a good portion of his time drinking bitters at the Come On Inn and thinking of ways to put her to rest with dignity, but inexpensively. What money was left could be stashed in the house on Esplanade, where there were plenty of hiding places. The fund would help get him started again when he returned from Altobello.

On the next Sunday, a chilly, blustery day, Moldenke's aunt's obituary finally appeared in the paper. He hurried into his clothes, ate a stale bear claw, hid the shoebox with the remainder of the ten mill under a paint-spattered drop cloth in the attic, and rushed to the car stop. It would all have to be brought off quickly, the ceremony and the burial. He would be leaving for Altobello in three days.

When it comes to the recent spate of impulse suicides among Bunkerville jellyheads, explanations vary. Some blame it on a localized effect of the "Voice of Bunkerville" radio broadcasts over station KUNK, which often make serious demands on listeners. Take Eliard Mozarti, a metals fabricator, who said friends bought him a wind-up radio last Coward's Day and each night since then he dialed in the Voice of Bunkerville from five to nine and when the order went out to kill himself he tried. Fortunately for him the hot bullet sizzled through his optic nerve, leaving him half blind but otherwise uninjured. He was up and about that very afternoon, chatting with close friends. KUNK put the idea in his head, so he claims.

The question is, can this kind of radio go on killing the weak of will for a lark? Can it take all jellyhead life from earth, one tortured soul at a time? Bunkervillians seem helpless under its spell, unable even to take their radios by the knobs and turn them off. Why couldn't they jerk the plug and silence the thing for good? Why do they let the broadcasts play on in their heads until they feel the heat of the bullet themselves?

Moldenke had to lean forward at a striking angle when he got off the streetcar to make headway in the blasts of polar wind and the wild whirls of dry snow in the streets. He was looking for the cold-storage unit, a shabby gray adjunct of the Charnel itself where the aunt's body was being kept under refrigeration. The building had once been a gymnasium and dormitory for young Christian men.

Moldenke stood outside in the cold, looking impatiently through the glass doors until someone saw him and opened one of them a crack. "Yes?"

"I'm here to pick up that older lady who was in the paper this morning. She died in the Charnel. Name of Moldenke."

The attendant opened the door fully. "Come in. You'd be...?"

"She's my aunt, a wonderful old gal. I loved her a lot."

"There *is* a storage fee to pay. Twenty-six hours. That's a half mil."

Moldenke peeled off two twenty-fives and gave it to the attendant. "That's a damned steep charge. I hope you pay your people well."

"Did you want her to rot?"

"Never mind. I'll take the body."

"How did you get here?"

Moldenke hadn't given a moment's thought to how he would move his aunt from Charnel Storage to wherever he would eventually bury her. There was no sense wasting money on a costly plot at Eternity Meadows. But he *could* afford a shovel and there *were* empty lots all over town. Would the ground be frozen and the digging impossible? He would have to think of an alternative.

"I came by streetcar."

"What will you do then, carry her?"

"I suppose so."

"She *is* very light, practically a skeleton. What you can do is let us cremate her. I'll make you a special offer. I'll do it myself on my lunch hour."

"How much?"

"Another quarter mil."

"No, I'll take her."

"She'll be cold and stiff for a while, you know."

"I figured as much."

"Come into the back, then. We'll get her."

The attendant led Moldenke down a cinder-block hallway into the "cool room," where the dead were stacked five or six high with I.D. tags wired to their toes. Snow drifted through the wide open windows, settling into little hills atop the frozen bodies. The males were stored on one side of the aisle, females on the other. Some of the protruding feet were blue and bruised, others as white as the snow itself.

"Where are the children?" Moldenke asked. "There must be dead children somewhere."

"We keep them separately. If we threw them on the pile, they'd slide off and we'd have a big mess. We keep them in bins, standing up, little shoulder to little shoulder."

"I understand," Moldenke said.

"This weather arrived just in time," the attendant said. "The lines at the ice distributing stations were growing rapidly longer morning to morning until the cold came. These bodies would smell to holy hell if they thawed."

The attendant stopped and held one of the tags close to his eyes. "Here we go. This is her." Being a recent death, she was very near the top, one layer deep. "You lift that top body up and I'll slide her out."

The attendant had no difficulty in pulling the aunt's body out from the stack and standing her on her feet in the aisle and holding her up by the neck. "See," he said. "It's easy when they're frozen, hardly any friction."

Moldenke was unsure just how to carry her. In his arms, like a stiffened child? She was no heavier or larger than a golf bag. He tried to pick her up, but he couldn't get a good grip. She slipped and fell to the floor. The attendant kept standing her up. "Why don't we strap her to your back?" he said. "I'll get some rope."

The attendant went off to a supply room, leaving Moldenke alone in the icy quiet with his frozen, naked aunt and the hundreds of bodies. He looked for the gold eye appliances that had kept her eyelids open. They might have had some value at a pawn. They were gone. He would ask the attendant about that.

He put his gloved hands around her frozen throat to keep her upright and closed his eyes in thought. How will I dig a hole in the hard ground? Where will I get a shovel?

Will they even let me on the streetcar with a frozen corpse strapped to my back?

The attendant returned with a length of strong twine. "This will have to do."

"I don't think it will," Moldenke said. Still, attempts were made. When a number of them failed, it was decided to quit the effort and think of another way.

"I could set her up on my shoulder like a pole."

"Good idea. I have an old rug in the office I don't want anymore. We'll wrap her in it and off you go."

"Wait, one thing. She had a pair of lid lifters in her eyes. They were gold. Do you have them? They may have been on the floor. They had fallen off."

"Lid lifters?"

"She was born with no muscles in her eyelids. They wouldn't open. She had these appliances made by a jeweler so she could see where she was going and what she was doing. Where are they?"

"There were no accessories when they brought her here, I can tell you that. If she spent any time in the waiting ward, the staff are a bunch of thieves. By the time we get them here anything worth anything is gone. They've been stripped. Sorry. Any effort you make to get them back will be futile."

"All right, I'll take your word for it."

The business of getting Moldenke's aunt rolled into the dirty, worn rug and tied off with twine went well enough and was over in a few minutes. The attendant hefted her to Moldenke's shoulder, making sure the weight was balanced. "There, that's the ticket. Should be smooth sailing. What will you do with her? You should've had her cremated."

"She always said she wanted to be planted in the earth like a flower bulb. I'll see she gets a decent burial."

When Moldenke was satisfied he had a good grip and that his aunt wouldn't tip too far down in front or back, the attendant opened the door to let him out. "Take care, Moldenke. The weather is changing badly. A storm's coming." Moldenke stepped onto the broken sidewalk and looked up at a dark sky. A rising, cold wind nipped at his face.

He thought better of taking the body to the house on Esplanade and digging a hole in the back yard. How could he dig deeply enough in frozen ground? If he buried her at all, it would be in a shallow grave and loose dogs in the neighborhood would dig her up. He was in a quandary until he thought of a place at the end of the streetcar line where the ground would be warmer.

Near Altobello, a suspicious red cloud dumped an extra-heavy dose of radio poison on the Black Hole Motel, occupied by five free people and ten jellyheads. "Had they continued to live there," Scientist Zanzetti said, "they could have contracted radio fever." The motel has since been deserted and Altobelloans are up in arms over the needless downwind danger. "Will the deadly clouds ever stop?" a druggist asked Zanzetti. "Not in our lifetimes," he replied.

When the streetcar stopped, Moldenke boarded with the rug-wrapped body. Though he tried his best to be careful, when he reached into his pocket for carfare one of his aunt's cold feet struck the driver in the face.

"For Christ's sake, man, what are you trying to do here? This is a streetcar, not a hearse."

Moldenke handed the driver three folded fifties. "I want to go all the way to the end of the line. I'll pay triple fare.

Look, the car is half empty. None of them care at all about anything."

"Four, you cheap son of a bitch."

Moldenke gave him four. "There, I hope you're happy—now I'm completely penniless."

"Sit in the far back, you stupid idiot."

Moldenke shifted his aunt from one shoulder to the other.

It was two hours or more before the streetcar reached the end of the line. By then, Moldenke was the only passenger. Not only had he soiled himself again, but the aunt had begun to thaw, dripping from both ends and wetting the rug.

The driver stood up and stretched. "This is it. City Dump. End of the line. Leave out the back with that stiff."

"Can you wait? It won't take long, just a small ceremony."

"You got another four? For that I'll wait maybe a half hour."

"I'm busted. Show some mercy. I can't walk all that way."

"Is that shit I smell on you?"

"I have a condition. It can't be helped."

"Get off."

Moldenke's shoulder, already sagging under the half-frozen aunt, sagged further. Not getting back to the Tunney would mean a night spent either trying to sleep on the frozen ground above the steaming pit or climbing down the slope to one of the ridges below where it was a few degrees warmer and provided enough room to lie down and sleep.

He knelt at the edge of the pit, bowed his head and said the only rhyming thing he knew. "Roses were red, violets were blue. You were a good aunt, and *I* loved *you*. Thanks for the money and the house. Bye-bye."

He untied the twine and unfurled the rug. There was little light other than a new moon. He could see only a hazy dark form rolling and bouncing down into the pit. The rug slipped from his grasp and followed her down, rising now and then on the pit's heat like a magic carpet.

In news from Altobello, the famous golfing jellyhead, Brainerd Franklin, received the heart of a free woman, Edith Farr, who was killed in a fall while visiting the Old Reactor ruins. Scientist Dr. Zanzetti performed the surgery. "Studies confirm the efficacy of human-jellyhead exchanges," he said. "Economically significant jellies like Franklin tend to reject the hearts of other jellies, but not of human females."

At age forty, Franklin was quite old for a jellyhead and too weak to walk the links and fire off those legendary drives. A donor was sought Bunkerville-wide, though none was found. It was thought that all hope for Franklin was lost, until a compatible donor became available. Now that the Farr heart has been transplanted, golfing enthusiasts are full of glee.

Just a day before his departure, for the little offense at Eternity Meadows, an officer of the court informed Moldenke that his stay in Altobello would be indeterminate. There would be no set date for his release.

Before going he would have to either board up or rent the house on Esplanade. Boarding it would be on the strenuous side if he tried to do it himself. There were a few tools in the shed, but he had no skills at measuring, cutting, or nailing. Hiring someone to do it would be expensive, take too long, and still, persistent thieves would eventually break in and help themselves. He asked around among his pro-labor friends if anyone needed a place to stay Someone suggested Ozzie, Moldenke's old high-strung associate.Moldenke found him in an alleyway on the poorer side of town.

sleeping on the ground, quilted over with burlap sacks and newsprint.

"Ozzie?" Moldenke kicked him lightly. "Wake up. I have a place you can live."

"I won't pay the going rate. It's way too high. Landlords are nothing but blood suckers. I will not pay it."

"I'm talking about my aunt's house on Esplanade. I'm being sent to Altobello for a while. I guess they need people there. I won't charge you any rent at all. Just watch over the place until I get back."

"There's a sweet deal, brother. I can't pass on that."

"Do you still have that pistol?"

"I had to sell it."

"All right. I'm leaving tomorrow. I'll put a key under the flower pot on the gallery. She's left a fund for fixing things when they break."

"Where is it, this fund?"

"Don't worry. Arrangements will be made. Send me a letter once and a while, general delivery, Altobello, and let me know what's what. That's all I ask. No rent will be charged."

"How long?"

"I don't know. It's indeterminate. A week, a year, the rest of my life."

Ozzie sat up and threw off the sacks. "I'll go on over there tomorrow. We're still picketing the Meadows today. You want to come with us?"

"I can't, really. My bowel is angry as hell. I'm afraid it'll happen again."

"Well, brother, I can't thank you enough. It's hard out here on the streets when it gets cold."

"Don't forget the letters. I'll be living in the house when I get back. So I want it to be kept up. Please let me know if anything goes wrong."

"Nothing to worry about, I guarantee it. I'm a clever person when I want to be. You know what I mean? I make friends easily, even with jellyheads."

"I do. I know."

"Good luck over there. I hear all that freedom can be pretty scary."

"I'll get by. I'll make the best of it."

As he waited in line to board the freighter *Pipistrelle* for the voyage to Altobello, Moldenke read the brochures made available to him. They covered the history of the liberation, gave general directions for getting around, lists of accommodations and streetcar schedules and the like. His plan was to settle down and make the most of his months or years of freedom. Maybe he would get a wild hair and sign on as a net mender on one of the big mud fish trawlers that went in and out of Point Blast Harbor or work on the docks unloading supplies from Bunkerville.

Zanzetti has completed a round of experiments that suggest jellyhead gel sacks contain living microscopic organisms and that these organisms may be communicating with similar life forms far beyond the moon.

He took a gel sack from his lab, set it on a stone in the sun outside, then attached wires to it and ran them into a simple galvanic device nearby. There he waited, sometimes as long as eight hours, for the signals to come in. He sipped tea and when the needles jumped and the green-faced scopes danced with lifehe rushed into action, jotting down figures and doing calculations. He said he doesn't understand the meaning of the signals but he is sure they come from somewhere beyond all the twinkles we see in the night sky. He said there was a general chatter going on between distant animated life and the organisms in the gel sacks.

Zanzetti tried for six months to break the code. When it is finally broken, he warned, the vision of our species may change entirely. "We may no longer view ourselves as the paradigm of all living creatures on this globe but as perhaps the lowest form of all, which is suggested by the newest evidence coming in through these sacks."

And why would minute life forms want to communicate with jellyheads? Zanzetti offered this explanation: "They're not communicating with jellyheads. They're communicating with gel sacks. The jellies are unaware of what is happening to them. They get impulses from the sacks and they act, for example, when they cut off the heads of their loved ones. That instruction comes from the gel sacks, which have a limited lifespan. Older jellies sometimes die of sack rot."

When asked how far off he thought the source of the signals was, he said, "This chatter is coming from at least ten thousand miles distance, a little shy of where we think the moon is. It defies belief that any kind of signal could travel that far. Our own devices are primitive by comparison."

On arriving at the Point Blast wharf, where newly freed people disembarked, Moldenke filled out all the forms necessary to get his pass card. He was issued light khaki pants and an equally light khaki waist-jacket. In another room he was fitted with underwear, linen shirts, a tie, sturdy boots, and several pairs of wool socks.

"Will I get a heavy coat? I hear the cold snaps here can be brutal."

"No coats. Wool shortage. Maybe in a few months."

"What do I do now? How do I get into Altobello proper?"

"Have some breakfast at Saposcat's. The Altobello car comes at noon. Catch it right in front. Show your card—it's free."

Moldenke headed down Wharf Street toward Saposcat's. Most of the residents of Point Blast were net menders or deck hands, often out to sea on one of the trawlers. But there were always free people coming there from Altobello to get commodities and mail sent over from Bunkerville. Their patronage allowed the Point to maintain a small Saposcat's with a limited menu.

Moldenke shifted his weight from heel to toe to keep blood flowing to his cold feet, waiting for the place to open. Along the sidewalk came a man and a girl of fourteen or fifteen, perhaps older. "I'm Udo. This is my daughter, Salmonella."

Udo carried a long, paper-wrapped package under one arm. The girl had a canvas bag over her shoulder. "Hello, mister," she said. "You look a little stupid. Are you?" She grinned. "Just kidding." Her teeth were mottled with blue, like a jay's egg.

"The name's Moldenke. I'm painfully shy, but not stupid."

"You a new arrival?" Udo asked.

"Just now checked in. Got my uniform, my pass card, my maps, but no coat."

"You'll freeze," Udo said. "Cold spells around here come up quick and hard."

"They said I might get a coat in about a month. The shortage should be over soon."

"Don't bother. They just say that. You'll never get one."

"The scrapple is good here," Salmonella said. "I really, really like it."

"They make it with pigeon, you know," Udo said.

"Whatever it is, I like it."

In the alleyway, outside the back door of the deli, a kitchen worker dipped pigeons into hot water to loosen the feathers for plucking then dressed the birds and tossed them into a bucket.

Udo shrugged. "Moldenke...you want to kill a jelly or two?"

"I've never tried it."

"It's a sublime experience. They're out there by the Old Reactor like herds of wildebeests. I pop them all the time." Udo hooked a thumb behind his canvas belt. "Didn't they tell you? You get time off for every ear valve you bring in. They got a valve return office in Point Blast."

"No, they didn't tell me that. And it wasn't in the brochures either."

"Well, let *me* tell you. Cutting off those valves is pretty disgusting. The stuff that squirts out'll make you gag. It's got cadaverine in it, and it smells like a dead body."

For Moldenke, the idea of killing jellies and cutting off their valves wholesale seemed a little distasteful. Besides, his sentence was indeterminate. How could he shave time from that?

"He's my daddy, but I don't love him for the way he loves killing jellies," Salmonella said. "It makes me sick."

Udo raised his open hand. "I'll slap you if you don't shut down that tongue of yours."

Salmonella folded her arms and looked away.

When Saposcat's doors finally opened, the three new acquaintances were seated at a booth. Udo's tightly wrapped package rested beside him.

A waitress took orders.

Moldenke said, "The mud fish, please."

Salmonella ordered scrapple with a side of fried kerd and a glass of green soda.

Udo waived the waitress off. "A bowl of meal, that's all."

Moldenke said, "I'm told new arrivals can get a streetcar outside that goes to the downtown, to the west side. I think I'll catch it. That's where I'll be going. It's the address they gave me at relocation."

Udo shook his head. "You'll wait all day. I've got my motor parked around the corner." He indicated the wrapped package. "We came here to get a new water tube for it, shipped in from Bunkerville. We're driving back to Altobello. You want to ride with us?"

Salmonella said, "I'm warning you. He's going to stop at the Old Reactor and shoot some jellies. He'll try to make you do it too."

"You want to shoot one, Moldenke? I got extra weapons."

"I wouldn't know what part to aim at."

"Not at the belly and not at the head," Udo said. "Huge stinking mess. They've got one gel sack inside the skull and eight in the belly. The one in the skull is what squirts out when you cut a valve. You don't want to puncture any of those. Aim for the upper chest. There's no sacks there. There's a heart. Some kind of heart."

Moldenke wasn't moved. "Thank you anyway. I think I'll maybe stay here in Point Blast, get a job net mending or working on the docks. It might be nice, close to the sea, the salty air, the sound of the waves."

Udo laughed. "Forget that. The menders and the dock workers formed a union, years of dues and apprenticeship before you get in. Nobody stays on the Point long. It's just a port. You come here to get things, you go back to the City. How long you here for?"

"Don't know."

"What offense?"

"Desecrating a grave. You?"

"I spit at the mayor's wife twenty years ago. Same deal: indeterminate. Salmonella was born here. She's freeborn."

Salmonella bared her teeth. "That's why I've got these blue spots."

"Most freeborn have the spots," Udo said. "Nobody knows why."

Salmonella said, "Freedom's fun. I can do anything. I don't care about the spots or anything else. I just don't care."

"Give me Bunkerville or give me death," Udo said. "That's what I think. I hate this place. Pure freedom is not what it's cracked up to be. See what it's done to my daughter? She likes jellyheads. She whines when I bust one. You heard her."

"He used to cut off the valves with a scissors, now he pinches them off with his fingers. It's sickening."

Moldenke gnawed on a crispy mud fish fin and considered his options. With little hope of getting on as a net mender or working on the docks, he thought it best to go on to Altobello and see how the free life would treat him.

"All right. I'll go along. I can't say I'll do any shooting."

Udo said, "It's the most fun you can have around here. You'll see. Now, hurry up and finish eating. The sun is up and it's getting hot. Let's get a move on." He ate the last of his meal. "Don't be dawdling, girl. Eat! You, too, Moldenke." He called the waitress over and showed her his passcard. "We're done. We're leaving."

As the three of them walked toward the motor with the sun ogling fiercely at mid-heaven, Salmonella recited a litany of complaints. "My shoes are too tight...My stomach hurts... That kerd was bad...The weather keeps changing."

Udo grew aggravated and slapped her to the ground. "You little bag of shit! Shut up and walk! I've had enough of you!"

"He treats me like a six-year-old," Salmonella sobbed. "He hurts me all the time. I really hate him."

Moldenke was surprised by the viciousness of Udo's slap but reminded himself that it was a parent's prerogative as a free person in Altobello to treat a child any way he wished. That he remembered from the brochures.

Undaunted by the slapping, Salmonella continued her complaints. "I can't walk any more. My legs are tired. I've got blisters."

Udo said, "Let's drag the little priss." He held the water tube under one arm and took Salmonella's hand. Moldenke grasped the other and they pulled her along. Once the motor was in sight she stood up straight and bolted for it.

"See what I mean," Udo said, "all the freeborn kids are like that. They piss and moan all the time. You and me, we've got some Bunkerville in us. She don't. That's the difference."

The temperature was above a hundred and ten already and Moldenke's stomach was full of oily mud fish and churning. "Is there a commode aboard your motor? I've got a bowel that gets angry."

"There is. Even got a few gallons of flush water."

Udo went into the big motor first and opened the windows to air out the living quarters. Salmonella said she felt feverish and asked Moldenke to feel her forehead with his hand. He did.

"Am I hot? Do I have a fever?"

"Yes. You feel very warm."

"Go take a nap!" Udo barked.

Salmonella went to her nook and flopped onto a cot.

Moldenke was tired. He lay on the divan for a while, then relieved himself on the commode. When he poured in the flush water he could hear it spattering into the dirt below the motor. There was a bucket of shredded issues of *City Moon* for wiping and a pitcher of clean water for rinsing the hands.

Udo spent what remained of the afternoon putting in the new tube and tinkering with the drive box and the boiler enough to get the motor purring nicely, all with just a screw driver and a box wrench. It was a "cranky" machine, he warned Moldenke, with worn shifters and bad bearings everywhere. The clutch was the devil to engage, the steering stiff, the brakes unreliable, and the boiler wearing out.

As he fumbled with the tube, trying to get the temperature adjusted exactly right, it came loose for a moment, long enough to scald him slightly on the chest. He fainted in pain but recovered quickly and had replaced the burst tube by evening. The drive to Altobello was underway.

A reporter for the *City Moon* stationed in Altobello was enjoying a glass of bitters in the Come On Inn when a jellyhead from the Old Reactor area came in, set her suitcase down, and claimed she had eaten nothing but grasshoppers since the Fourth of July. Her stomach was in an awful condition. She could feel their thorny legs scratching her alimentary canal. She had had a husband and seven famished children at home and had come to Altobello with their heads in a suitcase. She had done it to save them from starvation.

She asked the bartender for a glass of bitters. It was the only thing that would stupefy the hoppers and keep them dormant for a few hours. She said she had killed many of them with bitters before but that their eggs were always hatching. She believed there were at least ten thousand in her stomach and that some were moving toward one of her gel sacks.

She asked him to add a little peppermint and a few grains of sugar. That would make the concoction more potent. If peppermint wasn't handy, then a drop of mud fish oil would do.

The bartender, who had seen these desperate, hopper-eating jellyheads before, said, "I have a better idea." He poured two tablespoons of the essence of Jamaica ginger into a tumbler, added an equal quantity of piquant sauce, shook in a thimbleful of ground red pepper, emptied a jigger of heavy water on top, then sprinkled a few drops of tangle-foot over the mixture and handed it to the jellyhead. "Drink it quick," he said.

Without delay, the jellyhead swallowed the decoction.

"How do you like it?" asked the bartender, laughing under his breath.

The jellyhead's yellow eyes rolled in their wide sockets and tears ran out of them in cloudy streams. Her valves dripped gel, her mouth opened almost wide enough to swallow the barkeep and all his decanters then gradually grew smaller, her lips contracted, and the air rushed into her throat with a whistling sound. At last the barkeeper felt compassion and gave her a glass of water to cool her throat. When she was able to speak, she looked reproachfully at him and said, "See here, stranger, if that's the kind of stuff you give me for grasshoppers, I'd like to know what in the hell you'd give me if I had a tapeworm."

Having said that that she set the bloody suitcase beside the broken jukebox and left.

The reporter ventured to stand near the suitcase and jot down a few notes.

"What should I do?" the barkeep asked. "I thought they always left them at Saposcat's."

The reporter said, "With a thing like this it's best to do nothing. I'll write it up for the paper tomorrow. Take that suitcase and throw it off the public pier at Point Blast. Forget it happened. It's Coward's Day. They go crazy."

Udo's motor neared the Old Reactor and drove along a fenced in area that extended for miles. Inside, blue metal barrels were stacked in high pyramids. Most of them had burst at the seams and were leaking thick brown syrup. Udo said, "Jellyheads call that barrel honey. They put it on cuts and scrapes, like an ointment. They slick their hair with it. They might even eat it."

A jellyhead appeared in the motor's headlamps wearing a bone-colored straw hat and a soot-black coat that hung all the way to the ground. Udo braked hard. The jelly stood at the window, his face veiled by the sagging brim of his sweat-soaked hat. "You people going to the Reactor? Gonna do you some shooting?"

Salmonella came out of her nook.

Before opening his window, Udo said, "Bring me my weapon, girl."

"No."

"If I wasn't driving I'd smack her. Moldenke, go in the back. There's a satchel. Get my nine millimeter and bring it to me."

"All right."

"If you want to take a shot, there are a couple of other weapons in there."

Salmonella put her hands on her hips. "Don't be stupid, Moldenke. Don't shoot a jellyhead."

Udo turned and glared. "Shut up. Leave that man alone."

Moldenke brought the weapon to Udo, who opened the window and waved the niner at the jelly. "You by yourself out here?"

Cone-like concretions of dried jelly dangled from the jellyhead's ear valves.

"No, no. I'm going to bring out my friends." He curled two middle fingers toward his palm, raised his hand, poked the little and index fingers into the corners of his mouth and whistled shrilly three times—short, long, short. A sound like dry clay coming un-caked floated on the dark along with the sweet odor of wet rags as the jellies emerged from the shrubbery. When they appeared in the motor's dimming lights, Moldenke mistook their sewed-on smiles for friendliness. But in a canyon-low voice, one of them said he wanted Moldenke to put his arm out the window so that it could be touched.

"Don't do it," Udo said. "He'll squirt you with deformant. You won't have any skin left." Other jellies came out of the dark. "I don't like the looks of this bunch. They're about to go critical."

The one in the long coat shouted, "Why in the world do you want to be shooting us? We are the peaceful type."

Udo put the motor in low gear and crept forward. "Running over a jelly is well within the law here, but it could eat away at the tires." He revved the engine as a warning to the jellies standing in front of the vehicle. None of them budged.

Udo said, "I'm going to shoot a few." He took aim out the window and fired once. One of the jellies sank to his knees. "Oh, no, I hit him in the head." He jammed the motor into reverse and backed away as jellies ran to their dying friend. "I'm sorry I took the shot." He wheeled the motor hard right and re-set the finder for Altobello.

It was a slow machine, and the hard-scrabble road cut away at all the tires. "We need some heavy water," Udo said. "It's almost empty. There's a station on the By up here, not far. Big sign, says HEAVY WATER. Watch out for it."

"I will."

"Say something when you see it. I'm half blind at night."

"I will."

The night air whistled through the motor's open windows. Salmonella said she was cold and was going to bed. "Good night, Moldenke."

"Good night."

Moldenke slept, chin on chest, while Udo drove for an hour, until the HEAVY WATER sign came into view.

"There it is," Udo said, "heavy water." He angled into the station. There were only three or four motors, all shrouded in steam, filling up ahead of them.

Moldenke confessed he was anxious about living in Altobello.

Udo said, "You'll get accustomed."

Once they were inside Altobello limits, Udo pulled the motor up in front of the Wayfarer's Lodge. "Stay here tonight, Moldenke. Go look for a room tomorrow. There're plenty of places on the west side. Me and the girl, we're rooming at the Heeney Hotel over there. It's full, but there's a place down the street: the Tunney. They might have a room."

"I'll do that. Thank you for the ride."

A Bunkerville jellyhead who calls himself "Nick the Fuehrer"—a self-appointed, crusading detective—was arrested. Officers said the fifteen-year-old youth went too far this week when complaints poured in that he had been seen wearing a fuehrer veil, carrying a bull whip, and moving "very fast" through the City. After his arrest, the fake fuehrer protested to police that his only intent was to punish anyone seen breaking the law.

When Ozzie read in the *City Moon* that Darby "the Kicker" Nelson would be exploded on Friday, along with "Nick the Fuehrer," he made plans to attend. Nelson was a high-kicking jellyhead vandal who caved in four fender panels at Boxberger motors and lodged his foot a little too far into a windshield during one of his famous kicks. The next morning the police found him, the following day the courts judged him, and Friday he will die humanely.

Also exploding that day would be another jellyhead, Joseph Bloom, a self-described "sublime traveler" arrested along with his wife, Marvona, on the staircase leading to the second-floor bedroom of ten-term mayor Felix Grendon's home. Bloom defended his right to be there, producing a copy of a letter he had sent to the Mayor. The letter said, "Honorable Mayor, sir, I am a sublime jellyhead traveler and my old lady will be with me when I visit you. She will be wearing wraparound shades, 'cause she's got wraparound eyes. We have very important information you need to know. Stand by."

As things would have it, Grendon intervened in the arrest and agreed to talk to the couple for a few minutes before they were taken away. The press later learned that Bloom apologized to the mayor for his intrusion and said that in exchange for his freedom, he would reveal secret knowledge about gel sacks. "Marvona knows a lot, too," Bloom said.

Though the Mayor showed restraint and patience in listening to the delusional Blooms, they would soon face serious charges. While Marvona escaped punishment, Bloom was sentenced to death by detonation.

When asked how he felt about the harsh sentence, Bloom said, "Death is stronger than I am. It will blow me to kingdom come."

Most every day he sits in his cell playing a nose flute. A tea kettle boils on a hot plate. A small radio broadcasts Radio Bunkerville and he listens distractedly. In the jail yard, final preparations are being made to the three "boom" chairs where Bloom, Nelson, and the Fuehrer will sit.

Moldenke spent his first free night at the Lodge, sleepless. Twenty or thirty fellow arrivals, including an extended family of jellyheads, snored and farted and coughed in their bunks. Someone opened a window for air only to let in the stink of garbage and a pair of gulls who flew crazily in the dark. A wing struck Moldenke in the jaw with enough force to cause a bruise and swelling. He closed his eyes and covered his face with his hands, hoping for sleep that never came.

When the sun rose he put on his uniform and went out onto Arden Boulevard, but because Altobello's streetcars ran only every other day, he had to walk the twelve city blocks to the Tunney Arms, a rooming house on the west side. He didn't know Altobello well but had seen maps. Other new arrivals told him they'd heard that west-side jellyheads were popping out of alleyways or abandoned buildings or anywhere and spraying free men and women with aerosol deformant, scarring some of them for life.

Moldenke proceeded with caution, always looking around as he walked. The west side was unpainted and neglected, with shabby rooming houses offering free accommodations for new arrivals. The Tunney was no different. It was dilapidated outside and smelled of mold in the foyer. Along with the papers ordering him to Altobello, Moldenke showed the concierge his pass card and was assigned a room. "Freedom isn't free, mister," she said. "No bath, no kitchen, no nothing. And we're mostly full, too, so you're lucky there's a room at all. Eat and do your business on the street. And be careful. There're some bad jellies out there."

"So I've heard. I'll watch out. Is there a bakery anywhere near? I love bear claws."

"There's one over in the Quarter. If you need anything, the Quarter's where you'll find it. There's nothing around here but Saposcat's, privies, and rooms. There's a streetcar that goes there."

"Thank you for the information. Good night."

"If you have any trouble, please don't wake me."

"I won't."

The room was furnished with a bare cot; a plastic table; a wooden chair; and a small, splintery dresser. When Moldenke opened its top drawer out of general curiosity he found an aged copy of Burke's *Treatise on the Sublime and the Beautiful.*

There was a north-facing casement window that only opened halfway and couldn't close completely. But it let in just enough light that he could read himself to sleep. He had no interest in Burke's *Treatise* or anything else, but studying the impenetrable sentences and unfamiliar words first made his vision blur. He lay in the cot and held the book out to catch the best light. Doing so, he managed to read a few strings of words, leading him to understand that pain and pleasure were not opposite ends of a continuum, the presence of pain was not the absence of pleasure, and that indifference was the state of mind when neither was present.

Not long after he fell asleep and slept all day and most of the night.

———

It was revealed today in Altobello that Scientist Zanzetti locked himself into a shielded cubicle inside a small reactor of his own design. Standing with his head and shoulders visible in the tiny viewing cubicle, he could be seen staring distantly and playing with his fingers. He rarely spoke and then only to ask for barrel honey with which to smooth and groom the long silky black hairs of his chin beard. Every day he was furnished with a lead-lined frock and turban. Observers claim they could detect a cosmic and benign sadness in his misty, deep black eyes. Some thought he was intercepting messages intended for jellyhead sacks.

For breakfast the following day, Moldenke walked to a Saposcat's Deli close by, ate a bowl of scrapple, and drank a cup of strong tea, crowded as it was with a mix of free people and peaceable jellies, After that, he wandered around the west side, taking in the sights, such as they were. He learned quickly that bricks often fell from the tallest downtown buildings whenever a streetcar went by. He had to alternate looking up for falling bricks and looking down for the occasional sinkhole in the sidewalk. A broken ankle or a fractured skull would be disastrous. The hospitals closed only days after Altobello was liberated.

When he came to Liberty Park, a former urban green space that had apparently evolved into something of a jellyhead encampment and cemetery, Moldenke saw their underfed children roaming aimlessly, one of them chasing a rat. Another drank rain water from a puddle.

He walked generally and slowly past the grave of a jellyhead, who by custom were buried vertically and upside down, feet protruding from the earth. There was just a pile of toe bones left, a few toenails, and a gnarled shoe.

He picked up his pace until he was some distance from the Park, not far from the Quarter, which he was curious to see. He caught the Arden car at the next stop, showed his card, and took a seat. A few jellyheads across the aisle engaged in lively conversation. They seemed the harmless type, not likely to be carrying deformant. One of them leaned across the aisle and asked Moldenke if he would mind settling a dispute. "Glad to," he said.

"Tell us, in his famous *Treatise*, which concept does Burke say is the more compelling, that of the sublime or that of the beautiful?"

"I'm sorry to say, I haven't read much of it yet."

"You must. It's all the rage. Everyone's reading it."

"Thank you. I'll make a point of finishing it."

There was a crossing gate at the entrance to the Quarter. The car stopped and someone looking very official got aboard with a billy bat, slapping it rhythmically against his thigh. He walked slowly up and down the aisle, looking at passengers' faces, sometimes stopping to sniff the air around their seating area or to reach down and feel the passenger's heartbeat, perhaps to see if they might guilty of some infringement and feeling anxious. It was unclear to Moldenke what more the official was trying to determine, but whatever it was, Moldenke only received a brief glance with no hint of suspicion. When the inspection was over, the car rolled on to the Quarter. Knowing nothing of the place, he got off at the first stop, chose a direction at random, and began walking.

Photographers' bulbs flashed as two hundred jellyheads stood in the mud of City Park Wednesday night awaiting a miracle. They watched a nine-year-old jellyhead, Joseph Vitolo, pray at an improvised altar banked with pissweed and dandelion flowers, statuettes and dozens of guttering candles.

It was the sixteenth night the boy had seen a vision of the future in the rain clouds. He later told the press that in the vision he had foreseen a miraculous eddy opening beneath him, swallowing him entirely and admitting him into the ranks of the great saints and healers. The crowd saw no miracle yet, but several invalids and one or two with gel-sack rot claimed their condition had suddenly improved.

At seven p.m. the boy rode through the waiting crowd on the shoulders of a neighbor in a hard rain. Paralytics, others with crutches and bandages followed, trying to be near the visionary boy. The parade of drenched jellyheads went along in a semi-circle until the boy grew dizzy and almost fainted.

"Look! Look!" a rumor spread through the lot. "He is not getting wet. The rain doesn't touch him. It *is* a miracle. This is the one who has come to save us."

But those closest to the boy said he was as wet as anyone.

The concrete streets of the Quarter were cracked and sprouting weeds. Moldenke slowed down as he passed the Church of the Lark and its steeples. The odor of incense and beeswax drifted out into the street. Feeling a rumble in his bowels, an uncomfortable fullness, he went into the Church to get out of the sun and rest a few minutes, hoping to forestall an attack from the gut.

There were votive candles burning warmly in red glass cups. A Sister of Comfort swept the aisles. Another busied herself draping statuary with purple chintz. A third arranged paper lilies on the altarpiece. Moldenke breathed as deeply as he could; the scent of frankincense had a calming effect on him. He sat in a back pew to wait for the spasm in his belly to pass, but it only grew worse. He lay down and closed his eyes, falling into a dreamlike half-sleep where he lost control and soiled himself.

A light shake of the shoulder and a woman's voice brought him out of his reverie. "Sir, you'll find a public bath just down the street. Wash up there and have them boil those trousers."

"I am so sorry, Sister. It's something I can't avoid. I have an angry bowel, and I ate scrapple for breakfast."

"These things happen. Do hurry, though. We know the aide at the bath. He's a very nice young freeborn man."

Moldenke found Public House #6 only a block away. After showing his card and explaining the situation he was led by the bath aide to a small lavatory just off the vestibule and told to stand near the sink, remove his boots, socks, uniform trousers, and underdrawers. He did this while the aide watched. When he was finished the aide said, "Bathe in pool number one, then two, then three. These clothes will be clean and dry when you're done."

There were a few other bathers floating languidly in pool one, in water the color of tea, soaping themselves then diving under for a rinse. The water in pool two was cleaner, and three was spring fed and clear.

Feeling refreshed after a long soak in the pools, and with clean clothes, Moldenke ventured out onto Arden Boulevard. It had rained while he bathed, the streets were steaming, the air cooler, and there were reflective puddles on the sidewalk, each offering a blinding glimpse of the mid-day sun.

He stopped at the Tea Off, a free-talk salon, and looked through the window. Kerd cakes and tea were being served to small groups of new arrivals sitting at tables. For some it was an odd thing to speak freely, to exchange so much information without the supervision they'd known in Bun-kerville.

When Moldenke entered and showed his pass he was giv-en a slip of paper and a pencil. The host, who was busy brew-ing tea, said, "Print your name and list a couple of things you want to talk about. I'll put it in that jar."

Moldenke found a seat at the counter, signed the paper and wrote:

These are the things I would like to talk about. One: Who invented aerosol deformant and gave it to the jellies? Two: Angry bowel. What are the causes and remedies? Does any-one know?

The host collected the paper from him and put it in the jar. As Moldenke waited his turn, he drank tea, smoked Ju-leps and listened to the talk, which, though ranging wide, was orderly and polite. No one spoke out of turn or overlong. The host saw to that with a little church bell he carried on a thong swinging from his belt. *Ding-ding.* "All right now, that's enough about that," he might say.

A free man at another table talked about jellyheads. "They have a moving-picture mind. All life to them is a se-ries of snapshots with no chance for time exposure. That's why they can't think straight on any subject. Their minds are a bundle of transient impressions and confused ideas. What are we going to do about them?"

Ding Ding. "That's enough about jellyheads. Next...?"

A free woman said, "I wonder if it's true, what Burke said in his *Treatise*, that if we were watching a scene in a stage play in which a man was being brutally beaten, and some-one rushed in and yelled, 'There's a man being beaten to death outside,' most of us would rush out there to see the real thing."

The host rapped a table. "Proving what? Who wouldn't prefer a real beating to a staged one?" He pulled Moldenke's name out of the jar. "You're up, Moldenke. Table five. But first, here's the real question. Why do jellyheads have deformant and we don't?"

Everyone gave it thought, but there were no immediate answers.

Moldenke cleared his throat as he felt an uneasy twitch of his bowel. He worried that he wouldn't get to all his talking points before having to run for the privy.

There were no empty chairs at table five but someone at table four slid one over for him. He began: "One thing I'd like to bring up is aerosol deformant. Who invented it? And who put it on the City streets?"

A free woman said, "And the victims of these deformings? Who are they? Always handsome females."

The host, attracted by the discussion, stood near table five with a tray of empty tea mugs. "Zanzetti certainly invented it, but he claims he didn't give it to the jellies. One of his workers, a whistleblower, let them into the lab and they hauled off every can, the entire supply."

Another free woman asked, "What purpose is served by squirting us in the face with it? Why do they do it? Because we shoot them? Is that any reason?"

"They have deformant and we have guns," the host said. "Fair is fair. They're as free as we are."

"I'll tell you," a free man wearing thick eyeglasses and a horsehair wig said, "it's the difference between the sublime and the beautiful. Disfiguring beauty is a courageous and beneficial act. The horror of the victim's new face is very, very sublime. I'll take the sublime over the beautiful any day."

Moldenke raised his hand. "What about the angry bowel I have. How can I cure it?"

"Watch what you eat. Stay away from scrapple."

"If you can ever find any cheese, eat that."

The host looked at his watch and rang his little bell. "The hours do go by. It's already closing time. Everybody out. We'll take up these issues and lots more at noon tomorrow."

After the Tea Off closed, Moldenke walked to the day market at number nine Arden Blvd., where he'd heard there was a public privy. He bought a pack of Juleps from a tobacconist. "Why would anyone smoke anything else but Juleps?" the man asked. "Plain, menthol cooled, or cork tipped?"

"Plain for me," Moldenke said.

"Sorry, out of plain. Big shortage. Menthol cooled or cork tipped?"

"The tipped then…By the way, is there a privy around here?" Moldenke opened the pack and lit a Julep.

"Yessir, number seven. It's up there close to Big Ernie's Bakery."

"Thank you." Moldenke pressed his palm to his bloated abdomen, the burning cigarette between his fingers. "I never know when I might need to use it."

A few shops down, he passed Zanzetti Scienterrifics. A fat little clown-suited barker outside tried to engage passersby. Standing next to him was a pitiably deformed young woman wearing a sheer veil. "Been deformed?" the barker shouted. "Improve that face! We can make them younger, handsomer, and more expressive. We can restore deformant-damaged faces faster than all the paint and powder in the world. In one week, you can throw your veil away. Guaranteed."

After crossing busy Arden Boulevard, Moldenke smelled fresh-baked bear claws. The strong, sweet, floury scent probably meant the claws had just been taken from the oven. A green light blinked above the doorway of Big Ernie's Bakery. Forgetting for the moment that his bowel was angering, and passing the privy by, his mouth watered. He stepped inside the bakery, ordered a claw, and showed his card to the cashier, a young woman whose face had been deformed.

She saw him staring at her. "You wouldn't believe how pretty I used to be," she said. "A jellyhead got me by the Park. I was just walking by. What's the point of all this freedom when we've got jellyheads carrying deformant and using it whenever they want?" She turned sideways. "How do I look from the side?"

Moldenke felt obliged to respond, but words were slow in coming, and when they did they were tentative. "You don't look all that bad," he heard himself saying.

"Thank you, I suppose that's a compliment." She gave him the bear claw in a waxed bag. "My name's Sorrel—after the plant, not the horse."

"I'm Moldenke, from Bunkerville."

"How long are you here for?"

"Indefinite. Desecration of a grave. I'd rather not talk about it except to say it was an unavoidable accident. What about you?"

"Came with my father. He got life. They just needed a baker over here. I don't mind, though. I like Altobello. You can do what you want, except for the jellyheads. I hate them. If I had a gun I'd shoot my share."

Moldenke bit off a chunk of the pastry. It was crisp and sweet. "Oh, this is excellent an claw." He sat at a sunny little table near the front window and ate the rest of it.

Big Ernie came in from the back with a tray of fresh-baked claws and began lining them up in the display case.

Moldenke breathed in the fragrant smell. "Give me another one, please, to go."

Big Ernie backed his head and shoulders out of the case and stood his full height. "Welcome to Altobello, my friend. You're a free man."

"I can't say it's good to be here, but a person makes do. I suppose I'll look for some kind of work, employment somewhere. Best way to pass the time I hear."

"What's the point of working if everything's free? I got a passion for baking."

"I used to have a passion for the labor movement back home, but what's the use of that here? I do have a yen for these claws, though. They're far better than the best you can get in Bunkerville."

Big Ernie put a hammy hand on his hip and thought for a moment, then came to Moldenke's table and whispered to him, "Look at that poor daughter of mine." Moldenke glanced over at her. She was busy powdering her lumpy, misaligned cheeks. "A jellyhead did that, squirted her right in the face. No wonder she hates them. She wants a gun now. I tell her how hard they are to find. Can you do me a favor?"

"What's the favor?"

"Poison that son of a bitch for me, the one that deformed her. He goes naked with a big swinging donniker and wears a snap-brim cap. You can't miss him."

"I've never killed one. I've *seen* them killed with a firearm. I don't know about poisoning them. How would I do that?"

"Think of it like this: you won't be killing him...I will. You'll simply act as my agent. Here's an example. If you were squirted with deformant, would you blame the deformant or the jellyhead that squirted you?"

"The jellyhead, that's obvious."

"You see my point?"

"In a way, I do."

"The streetcars are running tomorrow. Catch the morning one to the Quarter, go to Smiley's Meats. Get a couple of sausages and put them on my account. Then walk on to Goody's Antique Hardware store for a tub of strong rat paste. Charge that, too. Take those sausages, split them open, and pack paste in there. I know that jellyhead loves sausages. There I was, coming back from Smiley's one day and the filthy thing grabbed a bag of hot links right out of my hand and ran off. I could see him crouched behind a tree, eating them. So go to the Park and leave them by that old dead tree."

"All right," Moldenke said. "I'll take care of it in the morning."

"Bring me the ear valves. If you don't have a knife, pinch them off with your fingernails."

"Right, I will." Moldenke's tone was laden with doubt.

Big Ernie smiled broadly and winked. "Little Sorrel'll owe you a favor..."

"All right. I'll take care of it."

Moldenke was on the afternoon car back to the west side feeling anxious. It wasn't in his nature to kill anything, even a jellyhead. He decided to distract himself that evening after an order of mud fish at Saposcat's by going to the Joytime Cinema, the only open one in the City, to see Misti Gaynor and Enfield Peters starring in *Who Puked in the Sink?*

Midway through the dull, slow paced film, Moldenke fell asleep. Just after its end, an usher awakened him. "Go home, fella. You've shit yourself."

"I'm sorry. It's something out of my control and it's getting worse." Moldenke yawned and stretched. "All right. But tell me, who puked in the sink?"

"It was the *plongeur*, the dishwasher. The wealthy partiers were leaving all those rich canapés on their plates and he'd been eating them. It made him sick and he heaved it all up right there into the three-chambered sink. Mystery solved. Now get on out of here. We're closing up for the night."

On the way back to his room, Moldenke ventured into a dark alleyway where he threw his soiled underdrawers into a trash bin. Fortunately the discharge in the theater had been light. His uniform pants were only lightly stained. When he reached his flat he hung them in the window to dry then sat naked all night, smoking Juleps and watching the progress of the half-moon through his window when the clouds and the swaying pants would let him.

It was an hour or two after getting into bed that he finally gave in to sleep and dreamed of Ernie's daughter coming fast toward him on a busy street, her hair wild and tangled and blown by the air she parted with her rapid walk. She looked as thin as death, expressionless as she came to him and locked him in a tight hug. They whirled around, which prevented him from looking straight into her ravaged face. He saw only parts of her—a cheek, an ear, and hair swept back like a comet's tail. His eyes were fixed in a stare at empty space. She said nothing, and her gaze never met his.

Employees at a streetcar terminal in Bunkerville watched in horror Monday night as a jellyhead fatally slashed her throat and stabbed herself repeatedly in the chest. Melba Morten, thirty-one, was dead on arrival at a hospital after the incident in the cafeteria of the terminal.

Randolph Scott, an off-duty police officer working as a security guard, struggled with the victim, twice trying to get the knife from her.

"She was split from one end to the other, screaming and gasping for breath," Scott said. "I tried to get a bandage on her, but I've never come across anyone so strong. She pushed me away."

Olga Pimental, cafeteria supervisor, said she heard Morten screaming. "I ran to see who it was and she was slashing her throat," she said. "She did it about three times. After she did it, she just stood there screaming. It sounded horrible."

After a cup of tea and a bowl of meal at Saposcat's the next morning, Moldenke cut through Liberty Park on his way to the streetcar stop and stepped into a mound of jellyhead stool hidden by leaves. There were no flies on it to give warning, even though the odor was unbearably foul, like something days dead. There were other mounds scattered around and balled bunches of wiping rags and soiled newspaper thrown about. It was a jellyhead toileting area.

As he waited at the stop, Moldenke scraped much of the stool from his boots onto the car tracks, but what remained smelled strong enough to get him kicked off as soon as he got on.

"Who do you think you are, getting on my car smelling like that?"

"Sorry, couldn't help it."

"Get off right now."

Moldenke jumped out of the car while it still moved, fortunate not to sprain his ankles. It was a long walk to Smiley's, and he was exhausted when he got there. He sat down outside on a concrete banquette under an awning and watched the comings and goings of Smiley's customers until he felt strong enough to go in. An elderly woman who passed him said, "I've never seen a maggot in Smiley's meat."

The market was cool and cavernous inside, the floors, walls, and ceiling covered in gleaming white tiles. There were several counters between the refrigerated cases, each with a long line. Moldenke chose one and prepared for a long wait. A free man in front of him said, "Holy Christ, man. I'm going to faint from that smell. Did you step in shit or something? Get in another line."

"All right. I'm sorry, I can't help it."

Moldenke moved to another line. When he finally reached the counter, he said, "Let me have two of your sausages."

"You got it. Two links on the way." The clerk wrapped them in waxed paper.

"Put them on Big Ernie's card."

"Oh, yeah, sure, Big Ernie's Bakery, downtown. Best claws in the Quarter. Him and me go way back."

The clerk disappeared through a rubber curtain. When it parted momentarily, Moldenke saw butchers at work sawing bones and cutting meat. A jellyhead boy in a canvas apron policed the floor, picking up fallen scraps and filling a wheelbarrow with them, which he emptied into the hopper of a sausage making machine, along with scoopfuls of pepper, salt, and other spices. At another station, a butcher emptied packets of gelatin into a vat of head cheese.

The clerk returned with the sausages. "There you are. Cook them a long time."

"Thanks for the caution."

Back on the street with the sausages, Moldenke asked someone how to get to Goody's Hardware. "Old Goody got deformed, you know. I'm not sure he's opened the store yet. It's only been a week or two."

"I didn't know."

"Some jellyhead gone critical barges into his store, squirts him, takes a sack of sulfur, fifty pounds of slug bait and a gallon of fly syrup. So Goody's out of all that. What do you need?"

"A tub of rat paste. I'll take the chance he might be open."

"All right then. Walk ten or twelve blocks north and there you are."

Moldenke felt the heat of the sidewalk through boot and sock and into the bottoms of his feet. The walk to Goody's was miserable and he was parched by the time he got there. After a long drink at a public fountain he sat down on a bench in front of the store and took off his boots. His socks were worn in places and there were little bleedings where shoe nails had pushed up through the sole and punctured the skin. He slammed the boots repeatedly against the concrete until the rest of the dried out stool fell off. When his socks had aired a little he laced his boots back up and went in under a hand-painted sign that read: NO JELLYHEADS.

In front of him was an opaque window where orders were placed, and another where they were picked up. Goody tended both wearing a rough, sagging mask scissored out of window curtains and held there by a headband.

He opened one window long enough to take the order then went about filling it. Only his wavering silhouette could be seen through the glass as he moved about. When the order was filled, Goody appeared at the pickup window to deliver it.

When Moldenke's turn at the window came he ordered a tub of rat paste. "The strongest you have. This is a big rat."

Goody went back to fetch the tub and Moldenke met him at the pickup window. "You can put this on Big Ernie's card."

"All right," Goody said. "He and I are good friends. His nuts click loud in this City."

"Sorry to hear about your deforming, Mr. Goody. It could happen to any of us I hear."

"Yeah, sure enough. That little jelly came in here in spite of that sign out there that says 'no jellies.' He ordered a sack of salts, and when I opened the window, he sprayed me all over my face, laughing, like he was having a lot of fun. I'm all scarred up."

Moldenke shook his head, which made his ears ring. "I guess that's the only fun jellyheads can have. Was he naked? Wearing a cap? Good sized donniker?"

"That's the one. The hat and the big peter."

Goody slid the tub of rat bait forward and closed the window suddenly, nearly crushing Moldenke's fingers. The lights dimmed. The store was closing abruptly for the day.

Moldenke shuffled out with a few unserved, complaining shoppers all rushing to the car stop at once. This time, with his boots clean, Moldenke thought he would be able to board the Arden car going to the Park. He did board initially without trouble, but along the line there was a kiosk and a stop sign between the exit from the Quarter and the entrance to free Altobello. An official stepped from the kiosk and entered the stopped car. He went up the aisle grumbling, checking pass cards. When he came to Moldenke he said, "You stink. Don't you think that offends the rest of the passengers? Get off now."

"Well, I'm sure it does offend them, but it's something I couldn't help. I stepped in jelly stool."

"In that camp in the park?"

"Yes."

"My young son fell face down in a pile when we were walking through there. They're worse than dogs, aren't they? Don't get off. It could happen to anybody."

The official signaled to the conductor to move on down the line, that everything on the car was fine.

After getting off, Moldenke sat on the curb to load rat paste into the sausages. He split the casing with his long, dirty thumbnail, parted the two sides, then used a stick to press the paste into the gap. When he turned to get up, he saw the naked jellyhead trotting purposefully across the street, tongue dripping with hunger, the large member swinging, the cap worn rakishly to the side. His hands, however, were empty. He wasn't carrying deformant.

Without slowing, the jellyhead snatched a sausage from Moldenke's hand and ran into the unlit Park. Moldenke followed at a chosen distance—not close, not far. It was getting dark and hard to see. The jellyhead slowed his pace long enough to eat half the sausage then raced on toward the old dead tree. Moldenke continued following. He had no idea how long it would take the jelly to die, and he needed the valves to show to Big Ernie.

The closer he came to the tree, the more distinctly he could hear groans of pain. The sickened jelly had curled up with his head close to a small campfire, his cap fallen off and smoldering. The bright blue eyes were open but unfocused. Moldenke kicked him a few times to be sure he was completely unconscious if not dead. He didn't want to reach for the valves until he was sure he wouldn't be bitten or sprayed with a hidden can of deformant.

Now, without a knife or a pair of scissors, it was a question of pinching off the fleshy valves with his fingernails. He knelt down and grasped one of the valves between his thumb and forefinger, sinking his long thumbnail into the flesh as far as it would go, then pulled the valve loose from its root. He did this to the other valve, put them both in his jacket pocket, and walked briskly out of the Park to the streetcar stop on Arden Boulevard, feeling relieved that his favor to Big Ernie was taken care of. When he showed his pass card, the conductor said, "You smell. Is that gel?"

"Yes. I was handling some valves and I've got gel on me."

"Sit in the back."

Moldenke gladly obliged and headed for the rear, holding on to seat backs to keep his balance as the car clattered off on the downtown line. It was early morning by the time it reached the stop a block or two from Ernie's Bakery. He'd walked only a few steps when his bowel gave early warning by passing dry gas. It wasn't all that urgent. He felt he could do his business with Ernie and still get to the privy in time.

Sorrel was behind the register as usual, her poor face heavily caked and painted. "Hello, Moldenke. You smell awful."

"Yes, I know. Is your father here? I have something to show him."

"He's in the back, proofing dough."

"I'll wait, then."

"You have the valves? Did you get the jelly?"

"I did. I have them in my pocket. That's what you're smelling."

"Let me see them."

Moldenke took the two valves out of his pocket and displayed them in an open palm. "It wasn't easy getting them off. I had to dig in and pull hard. They came out with the roots. There wasn't anything to cut them with."

"It gives me the chills to look at them. Let me go get Daddy." She gave Moldenke a bear claw.

He sat at the table and waited quite a long time. Eventually Ernie came out, dusted all over with flour. "She tells me you got the little demon."

Moldenke held out the valves. "There they are."

"Nice work. We're glad to know he's dead and gone. I'd give you a reward, but everything's free here." He turned to Sorrel. "Like my little girl there who's free to do anything she wants to." He winked at Moldenke. "She might get sexy with you, who knows?"

Sorrel lowered a veil over a withered, blushing cheek and put three or four claws into a bag. Ernie delivered them to Moldenke's table, bent over, and whispered, "Her face is no good anymore, but the rest of her is fine. Why don't you ask her out on a date? You can use my card. Go to Saposcat's. Eat some food, drink some bitters. Have some fun."

Sorrel overheard. She smiled and turned away.

"Maybe," Moldenke said, giving her his awkward little salute. "When I get settled. I need a little time."

Ernie and Sorrel followed Moldenke out onto the sidewalk and waved goodbye.

Zanzetti Scienterrifics has produced the first "preternatural boy." He was born in the seventeenth month of fetal development, delivered by a "treated" jellyhead mother andhoused in a basement room of Zanzetti's Bunkerville laboratory complex, kept comfortable with air coolers and de-humidifying units. Prone to fungal ravages of the epidermis he was otherwise sound and healthy.

The *City Moon*'s headline was: FIRST 'GODBOY' BORN IN BUNKERVILLE

Zanzetti was quoted as saying, "His brain will be a whopping twelve pounder, if he matures. We'll harvest it, keep it alive in a saline and sugar solution, and see if we can get it to help us think better."

"The paper called him 'Godboy,'" a reporter said. "Are we to draw any conclusions?"

Zanzetti shrugged and looked upward. "Gods have been around since ancient times. We expect this one, like the others, to grow up and change the world for better or worse. I'm a scientist, and I say, eventually, why not now?"

One afternoon Moldenke went to the Saposcat's on Arden for lunch. He found Udo and Salmonella there. Salmonella ate mud fish, picking them up in her hands and chewing them through, even the softened bones. Udo drank tea, ate nothing, and read the *City Moon*, which arrived in Altobello with day-old news. A reader had to allow for recent developments, especially if they related to events in Altobello, which had no newspaper.

"Well, yippie," Salmonella beamed. "It's Moldenke. Sit with us."

"Look at this," Udo said, tapping the paper with his finger. "Some kind of jellyhead show over on the east side tonight. It says Brainerd Franklin'll make an appearance. Let's go. Let's all go."

Salmonella placed her hand on Moldenke's knee. "Come on. Come with us. Franklin's that famous golfer. Daddy won't shoot him. He's too famous."

"It'll be fun," Udo said.

"All right, I'll go along."

Salmonella clapped her hands. "Yippie!"

Udo folded the paper and swatted a fly on the window sill. "We'll pick you up in front of the Tunney at half-past seven."

———

Moldenke slept the afternoon away in his room, awakened at six by the distant sound of the *angelus* ringing in the tower of the Church of the Lark. He put on his uniform and boots and combed his hair without a mirror, glad he'd had a chance to sleep, to store some energy for the show.

Udo's motor pulled up exactly at seven thirty. "Get in. It starts at eight sharp."

Salmonella, sitting in the passenger seat, slid over to give Moldenke room to sit. "Promise you won't shoot one, Daddy?"

"Shut up you little twit. Quit hounding me. They don't feel pain like we do."

Salmonella brushed back her hair with a quick motion and let her tongue part her lips into a smile. "What about you, Moldenke? Do you know if they feel pain?"

"They lack consciousness, it says in the brochures. They took it out of their own heads and put it into machines. That's what turned them into jellyheads way back when. So they really don't feel much of anything."

Udo placed a hand around the grip of his niner to still the tremor, then rubbed the weapon with an oiled cloth.

Moldenke ate the second bear claw, soggy now and soaked with the fishy oil they were fried in, then lit a Julep. "I'm worried this won't go well," he said. "There might be trouble."

Udo shrugged. "Trouble? No chance of that. So what if I wax a few jellies. People used to kill chickens and fish, didn't they?"

Moldenke retrieved a long-stored memory of killing a chicken. It had happened when he was visiting his late aunt's country home, where she kept a dozen free-roaming pullets. One spring day she asked him to go out and kill one and give it to the cook to fry. "He makes the most sublime spring chicken. We'll have it for supper tonight. You kill it, he'll pluck it."

Moldenke went out and snatched the legs of one of the pullets and held it upside down. He took the head in his hand and pulled at it ineffectively, never hard enough to take it off. A pair of garden shears would probably do the job faster and better. He went to the shed, carrying the bird by the feet. The shears hung on a nail in the wall. He closed the door to keep the pullet from escaping and chased it with the shears, finally trapping it in a corner and closing the dull blades across its neck. Rather than shearing off the head cleanly, the neck merely folded flat between the blades, crushing the bones.

"I did kill a chicken once," he said. "The wrong way. The way I thought was the smartest, and the chicken suffered a slow death. I could taste it in the meat when we ate it for dinner. It was off flavor."

Udo said, "Enough blather. It's almost dark. Let's go see that show." He set the finder for an address on the east side and the motor rolled toward the bypass.

Only days ago it was learned that near the Old Reactor, a jellyhead village of odd little mushroom-shaped dwellings has sprung up. Some are hemispherical, some barrel-like, some oblong, and at the top of each is a bucket of gel sacks, tending to prove Zanzetti's theory of interspatial communication between the sacks and distant life.

Should free people take action? "No, not yet," the scientist said. "Let me break the code, see what they're talking about. There could be a way to distort the impulses from the sack and get the jellies to behave themselves and work for the general good."

Zanzetti's experiments will continue, and periodic reports and memoranda on his progress will be issued until the code is broken. In related research, the great scientist has pioneered a process for partially reviving newly dead jellies and putting them to work. Though he is guarded in any release of specifics, he does say that it involves the use of electromechanical stimulation of the cranial gel sack. All the mechanics and electronics are packed into a small box the size of a deck of cards worn at the back of the neck. The technique has worked on test subjects in the laboratory, Zanzetti says, and he hopes to begin additional trials very soon. "They won't be like they were in the full bloom of life," he warns, "but put them in front of a punch press or a milling machine and they'll work it all day and expect no wage. They're also non-vocal, so they'll go about their tasks quietly. And they don't eat, so they won't require feeding or toileting facilities."

Zanzetti proposes to use them in performing menial tasks. "They'll sweep the floor, they'll draw your bath, they'll chop vegetables and wash windows. There's no limit to the little jobs they can do. At bed time you just remove the box and they're out like a light, dead to the world. Let them sleep in the garage or the cellar."

After parking the motor, Udo, Moldenke and Salmonella stood on the stoop of a lap-sided, two-story house that had recently been painted, in contrast to the dilapidated buildings on both sides of it and all through the old neighborhood. There were a few streetlights burning dimly on low current.

Udo rang the bell. They waited in the heat until someone opened the shutters, raised the shade, and parted the curtains of an upstairs window. It was a woman with a slender face and a fair complexion. She blinked in the sun and held a hand over her eyes. Curls of black hair fell in ringlets to her shoulder. She opened the window, smiled down from the folds of the muslin curtains, and pointed at a service alley running along the side of the house. "Are you looking for the jellyhead show?"

"Yes, ma'am," Udo said.

"There's ten or twelve of them in my basement, living down there like bats. Here I am with the best kept house as far as I can see in the only decent neighborhood in Altobello, and look what moves in. Now they're putting on a show."

Udo placed his hand over his heart and patted the side of his weapons satchel. "We'll take care of them, ma'am."

"Let me thank you in advance," the woman said, closing the window and drawing the shade.

"Daddy, don't shoot them."

"I agree," Moldenke said. "Let's just watch the show."

"Tell you what," Udo said. "We'll watch the show and then I'll take care of business and get some valves after it's over." He went up the alley and through a low door.

Moldenke looked at Salmonella. "I'll go with him. You stay out here."

"No, I want to see the show."

"All right," Moldenke said. "If he starts shooting we'll leave."

Salmonella, wary, followed Moldenke down the alley and into the basement.

There were wooden folding chairs arranged in rows of ten and a small plyboard stage lit by a dim bulb hanging from a joist. Udo was sitting in a front row seat. A jelly at a table near the doorway greeted Moldenke and Salmonella. "Come in. The show is free tonight. Brainerd Franklin's here. It's a special appearance. He's going to work with needles."

Salmonella asked, "What does he do, balance them on his nose?"

"No, no, not at all. Let me take you backstage. You can ask him yourself. He is a treasure to us, to our community. I'm his assistant."

Bed sheets had been draped over a rope to define the back of the stage. It took only a few steps to get there. Franklin sat on a wheeled stool at a vanity table. He wore a white terrycloth bathrobe, the hood pulled over his head. When he saw the backstage visitors, now including Udo, he spun around and wheeled closer to them, extending his hand palm down, as if expecting it to be kissed. Moldenke took the hand awkwardly for a moment and released it. When he did, it fell back and struck the leg of the stool. Brainerd winced then coughed up a wad of clear gel.

In a whispered aside, the assistant said, "Careful now. He's very delicate in this state."

Udo's bloodless lips pulled back into a snarl. "All right, Franklin, let's get on with the show. My girl here wants to know what you do with the needles."

Franklin's ear valves were erect and dripping gel. "It's almost show time, my friends. Please join the audience. You'll see what I do with the needles."

Ten or twelve jellies had taken their seats in front of the stage, set with a cane-back chair and a bowl of silver needles on a small table. Franklin appeared from behind the bedsheet curtains, lifting himself along like an ape, using his fists as feet, and took his place in the chair.

His assistant ambled onto the stage. "The great golfer is in a trance state now and will work with his needles."

As Franklin's head came to rest on his chest, the light was turned off.

"I don't like this at all," Udo whispered. "I'm going to start shooting in a minute. That son of a bitch might go critical."

The light sparked on again. Franklin stepped out of the chair and heaved himself forward, closer to the small audience.

The assistant said, "It is his pleasure now to show you his needlework."

Franklin turned about and lifted the hem of his robe. There was a low hum of excitement in the room. When the robe was raised high, everyone saw a massive scrotal sack trussed with sewing needles placed either sideward or upward and yielding a good bit of blood.

Salmonella shrieked.

Udo stood with an audible snap of his knees, his niner in hand. "That's enough. What kind of show is this?" He took aim at Franklin. "I don't care how famous you are, you bucket of jelly. Look what you're showing to my daughter."

Salmonella said, "I'm going, Daddy. I'm going outside," and left the basement.

Moldenke waved his hand at Udo. "I'd think again before doing Franklin. His fans are legion. They could come after you."

Udo lowered the weapon. "Good point, Moldenke."

Franklin let his robe hem fall and backpedaled from the stage.

Udo turned to the seated jellyheads. "I'm not going to do Franklin, but the rest of you, kneel down and bow your heads."

Franklin's assistant was the first to kneel. Udo shot him in the back of the neck. Moldenke made for the door, quickstepping all the way, never looking back.

The jellies in the audience had remained in their seats, petrified, valves dripping but quietly accepting of their fate. Heads were lowered as Udo went up and down the rows of chairs firing into neck after neck, killing eight. The ninth was a young female not much older than Salmonella who lay on her stomach with her neck arched. "Thanks," Udo said, "for making it easy." He placed the end of the barrel very close to the raised neck and fired once. The jelly girl went limp. He stood over the body. "You're still twitching." He fired another shot just as her head snapped backward in a spasm. The shot was too high and entered the skull, letting out a stream of steaming gel.

Udo fumed. "What a stink. Let me out of here." He walked around the basement with a pocket knife, trying to keep his breathing to a minimum to avoid the odor of so much gel, snipping off ear valves and putting them into a bag. "This is what, ten sets? Hell, man, that's some real time off."

Franklin peeked from behind the curtain and wept. "You've killed some of my fans." He blew his wide nose into the shoulder of his robe. "I can tell you this about your future: there will be a time when you need fans and you won't have them."

Udo thought about that prediction for a moment. It made no sense to him. Why would he ever need fans? He gave a second thought to shooting Franklin. He curled his finger a bit more tightly around the niner's hair trigger.

Moldenke and Salmonella continued to sit in the motor waiting. The black-haired woman opened her upstairs window. "I heard the shots. Did you get them all?"

At that moment Udo came out of the basement. "All but one, ma'am. Franklin. He's too famous to kill."

"What will I do with all the bodies?"

"Don't know, ma'am. That's your business. Get that trussed up Franklin to help you."

The window slammed shut and the shade was pulled down.

An estimated seven thousand gallons of so-called barrel honey spilled into City Canal near Bunkerville today. A freight wagon overturned, ruptured, then fell from a bridge into the Canal. The release of the dangerous "honey" caused a yellow cloud to spread over the City and two thousand were evacuated from their homes. Because Bunkerville uses City Canal as a source of drinking water, the pumping facilities will be closed for forty-eight hours as a precautionary measure. The importation of barrel honey from Altobello's Old Reactor area is forbidden by Bunkerville ordinance, punishable by detonation.

A rumor spread in Altobello that Franklin would be playing an exhibition round in Liberty Park. The weedy, old, pre-freedom course there had been restored by jellyhead labor over a period of weeks. Word of mouth spread, and there was intense interest and anticipation.

Moldenke made a point of attending, though he missed the first eight holes. Udo and Salmonella were easy enough for him to spot in the crowd at the ninth. She wore a brilliantly pink dress and black patent pumps. Udo, in his uniform, was almost indistinguishable from others in uniform. Sorrel was there, too, with Big Ernie, who carried a cloth-covered basket of bear claws.

Moldenke tapped Udo on the shoulder. "Udo."

"Moldenke."

Moldenke smiled. "Salmonella. You look nice."

"Thank you, Moldenke. Why are you here?"

"I want to see Franklin play."

Udo said, "I turned in the valves, ten of them. That's three months off my time."

"Which is indeterminate, like mine. So it doesn't make sense to think you'll be getting time off no matter how many valves you turn in."

Salmonella tugged at Udo's uniform. "Moldenke's right, Daddy. That shows how stupid you are."

"Quit tugging on the uniform, you little shit." He gave her a nasty thump on the ear with a snap of his middle finger.

"Ouch! I hate you!"

Udo pushed Salmonella backward. She nearly fell, until Moldenke stopped her and stood her up. She began to cry and rub her eyes.

Udo suddenly back-paced a few steps then turned and lost himself in the crowd.

Moldenke said, "Hurry up, run after him. Please, go with your father."

"He's gone," Salmonella said, "and I'm glad. I'll stay with you. You can take care of me."

"Where's your mother? Who's your mother?"

"I don't know. He didn't talk about her."

"An uncle, an aunt, anyone else who might take you?"

"Nobody."

"I don't have much room in my room, and it's all I can do taking care of my angry bowel. You should go to the Youth Home. I'll take you there tomorrow. You can sleep on my floor tonight."

There was a roar from the crowd when Franklin approached the ninth hole, then a lull as he studied the lie of his ball about ten feet from the cup.

"I can't see," Salmonella whined. "Pick me up." Moldenke lifted the bare-boned girl to his shoulders easily. Her legs cradled his neck and she rested her chin on the top of his head. "That Franklin sure does dress sharp."

Moldenke stood on tiptoe to see over the crowd. Franklin looked resplendent in a yellow silk blouse, checkered shorts, and a spiffy long-billed cap. His trainer was never far from him, shouting encouragement. Franklin crouched low and sniffed along the green from the ball to the cup. "Atta boy!" the trainer shouted. "Easy putt! Easy putt!"

His caddy slid a shortened club from the bag. Franklin jerked it from him, sniffed it thoroughly, then addressed the ball. When he did so, observers in the crowd saw blood-spotted needles protruding from the rear of his shorts. The putt went off with a *thwack* and the ball dropped into the cup. Franklin pounded his chest and grinned for the crowd. Anyone familiar with his style knew what came next. His handlers formed a circle around him to keep the business private. When the circle broke and the group moved on to the tenth, a groundskeeper would be seen shoveling Franklin's steaming stool into a bucket as his handlers pulled up the golfer's shorts.

Moldenke smelled bear claws just then, a moment before Big Ernie and Sorrel came along giving them away. Sorrel stood close to Moldenke, handed him a bear claw, and whispered, "Let's have dinner tonight at Saposcat's, if Dad will let me. He beat my last boyfriend half to death for patting my behind, sent him to the crazy house a drooling idiot."

Moldenke was caught off guard. "I've been to Saposcat's. I love their fried mud fish. But, you know, my bowel feels angry. I'd best stay in the flat tonight. I have this girl to take care of, which is another complication. Her name is Salmonella."

Salmonella beamed at the attention. Her father had never introduced her formally to anyone. "I think I'm named after a little fish from olden times."

"The salmon," Moldenke said. "It used to go up rivers. People ate them."

"Another time then?" Sorrel asked.

In truth, Moldenke was repulsed by her facial deformities and doubted he wanted to be seen in her company at Saposcat's or anywhere else. Yet her body was very easy on the eye, her hair long and radiant, her breasts modest but likely well-nippled, her buttocks perfectly formed. It would be a bit much for him to ask her to wear a veil. Still, he was on the verge of politely making that request when she said, "Don't worry. I'll wear my veil."

Under that condition, Moldenke agreed to meet her at Saposcat's at seven.

Salmonella said, "Count me in. I love their fried kerd. The mud fish's not bad either."

"She'll have to come," Moldenke said. "I've got her for the night."

"That's okay," Sorrel said. "This *once*."

Big Ernie appeared out of the crowd with an empty bag. "Everybody got a claw. Let's go, Sorrel."

"Listen, Father, Moldenke and I will be going to Saposcat's tonight. Do you have any objections?"

"As long as he's a good boy and keeps his hands off." Ernie winked at Moldenke.

"Shouldn't be a problem," Moldenke said.

Salmonella clapped her hands. "I'll be the chaparral."

"You mean chaperone," Moldenke said.

"You teach me stuff, Moldenke. I like that."

Big Ernie came along and patted Salmonella on the head. "Who's this little gal?"

"Her father ran off. I'll take her to the Home tomorrow."

Big Ernie looked down at Salmonella. "That's the best place. It's full of young free people like you."

Two Bunkerville celebrities, the actress, Misti Gaynor and the writer, Sissy Peterbilt, have died in unrelated accidents.

Gaynor's sodden body was discovered at about five a.m. yesterday. Sometime the night before, during an unpredictable downpour, she had slipped, fallen, or collapsed into the three-foot-deep gutter ditch that runs the length of Esplanade Avenue. It is estimated that the gutter quickly became a gushing stream of rain water, engulfing the actress and carrying her more than a hundred yards, where she was found dead.

Peterbilt was crushed when she stopped to gawk at an excavation near a smelter and was buried in eighteen-pound blocks of pig iron, which fell on her. It had been reported that she was hard at work on the life story of Scientist Zanzetti.

At seven sharp, Moldenke and Salmonella stood outside Saposcat's, waiting for Sorrel. The weather had changed suddenly after Franklin's exhibition, and a warm, bright day had given way to sudden downpours.

Salmonella complained, "I'm getting wet. The awning is full of holes."

"An umbrella would be good to have," Moldenke said. "Or even a rain hat. You can't get anything here."

"Don't bring me to the Home. Why can't you look after me? I'm afraid of the Home. There's jellyheads there. I could get deformant in my face. They sneak it in."

"Don't be silly. I'm sure they'd confiscate it."

Moldenke looked up and down Arden Boulevard. "Try to behave. She'll be here any minute."

Passing motors kicked up a mist of dirty water that settled on everything. One of the motors, a deluxe model K-10, glided to a stop in front of the Deli. A chauffeur dashed out and opened the rear door.

"That's Franklin," Salmonella said.

The golfer slid out of the seat with a broad grin, his legs spread widely, wearing a well-tailored mohair jacket, starched shirt, a gold lamé tie, and boots made of animal skin. A handler held an umbrella over his head and escorted him into Saposcat's.

At that moment, Moldenke saw a streetcar round the terminus at the end of Arden and screech to a stop half a block from the Deli. He told Salmonella to stay put while he met Sorrel at the stop. He could already see someone getting off wearing a macramé veil.

"Sorrel. Here I am. Hurry, your veil is getting wet."

"What a ride," she said. "The car ran over a jellyhead baby. The mother threw it under the wheels and ran."

"That happens all the time."

"It was quite a delay. That's why I'm late. They had to clean up all that stinking goo on the tracks."

"I like your veil. It's very pretty, even wet."

"I made it myself. I can smell, I can see, I can eat without offending."

"Let's get inside. You'll never guess who's in there. None other than the famous Brainerd Franklin."

Sorrel said, "Oh, that should be interesting. I hear he smells bad up close. I hope we don't get seated next to him."

A sandwich board set up outside the front door listed the night's specials: *Scrapple, Kerd, Meal, Mud fish, Sturgeon (seasonal), Trotters.*

"It all sounds good to me," Salmonella said.

Although the place was only moderately busy, many of the tables were reserved for Franklin, his handlers, fans, guests, and the visiting Bunkerville press, so there were only a few unoccupied. Sorrel chose the one farthest from Franklin, who was answering questions shouted at him from the press.

"Do you jellies believe in an afterworld?"

Franklin answered in slow, deliberate fashion, as though he were drugged. "After what? Oh, I get it. Sure, yeah, of course. I hope so, anyway. A jelly doesn't any more want to be dead than you do."

"Why does golf need a jellyhead player?"

"Ask a simpler question. And get me another plate of fish."

"What's a sand wedge for?"

"To eat, I think. Isn't it? My trainer always made peanut butter ones for me when you could get it, and bread."

"Who makes your boots?"

"The Franklin Bootery, back in Bunkerville. I own it. I'm rich. It feels good. It's one thing to be a poor jellyhead, but a poor free man? It must be awful."

"Do jellies believe in any gods?"

"Are you kidding? No god ever gave a jelly a break. I dig Masonry, though. I've got a scooter and I love to ride in parades, especially on Coward's Day."

"Do you have a philosophy of life?"

"A what?"

"Like a guiding principle, sort of a rule or rules that you follow?"

"Life is a bogey, not an eagle. We are always one stroke over, always in hazard. Fairways turn foul, every tee off ends in a slice. The game is forever uneven, the score is never settled. I often feel under par, and sometimes vengeful, which is why I hardly ever carry aerosol deformant on my person."

"So, where do you go from here?"

Franklin bent over and held his abdomen. "Excuse me, please, but it's time for me to make for the potty. I'm all loaded up. Got to dump it."

Two handlers grasped Franklin by the elbows and walked him to the gutter outside. Even at that distance, and with the doors closed, Saposcat's patrons could hear Franklin's apish grunting and smell the odor of his stool.

"What a disgusting display," Sorrel said.

"It sounds like an angry bowel," Moldenke said.

Salmonella held her nose. "That is bad, bad, bad."

Moldenke wanted things to go well, despite Franklin's display. He studied the menu with seeming calm. "Mmmm, the river sturgeon looks good."

Sorrel summoned a busboy. "Tell someone to turn on the ceiling fans. It smells awful in here."

"Yes ma'am."

After switching on the fans, a waiter came to the table, pad and pencil in hand. Sorrel said she needed a minute or two. "I'm torn between the mud fish and the kerd."

Salmonella elected to have the mud fish.

Moldenke ordered sturgeon steaks. The waiter shook his head. "I'm so sorry, these steaks are driftwood-grilled out-doors and can only be served when the weather is fair."

"All right, give me the kerd with a side of the trotters and a pint of bitters."

Sorrel finally made up her mind. "I'll have the trotters too, and a glass of bitters."

"Does the girl want anything to drink?"

"Yeah, I sure do," Salmonella snorted. "I want some green soda."

"I'll get that order in right away."

When the drinks arrived, it seemed to Moldenke the right time for conversation. "Sorrel, tell me, what is your favorite color?"

"Black. I like black best."

"Besides ugly, you're pretty stupid," Salmonella said. "Black isn't a color. Everybody knows that."

Sorrel was offended and Moldenke grew impatient. "The whole idea of color is a human concept, a word. That's all. Drink your soda and hush."

Even through Sorrel's macramé veil, one could see her face flush in anger.

"Her father abandoned her," Moldenke said. "I took her in for a night. Call me soft-hearted."

"She belongs in the Young People's Home."

Salmonella twirled her hair anxiously. "Don't listen to that, Moldenke. I *do not* want to go there."

Just as the waiter set the plates on the table, someone from the press yelled out. "He's had a heart attack! The great golfer is dying!" Six or seven of his handlers carried Franklin and placed him in his motor, which sped away. It was rumored that he would be taken to his yacht—the *Blue Crab*, docked at Point Blast—where his personal physician had been stationed.

The Altobello Young People's Home, run by the Sisters of Comfort, was a walled fortress of youthful freedom, a freedom thought by some to be more like neglect. Ordinary young people lived largely unsupervised among wild young jellyheads, who were ever ready to bare their blue teeth, spit at you, or squirt you with deformant. With the shape of an octagon, the Home surrounded a central commons, where young people of both sexes were set free without food, cloth-ing, or shelter. It was everyone for him or herself.

A healthy grove of pines grew there on a rise above a siz-able fishing pond, an apple orchard, several acres of rich soil set aside for crops and enough of a meadow to graze a few animals. It was thought that in those surroundings and sup-plied with the tools of survival, that the young people would learn that life is what you make of it.

Salmonella was glum and quiet as she and Moldenke rode the streetcar. He tried to both excuse himself from what he was about to do and at the same time explain why he was doing it.

"First of all, you're not my child. Your father abandoned you. The Home is where you belong. If I see your father, I'll insist he come and get you."

When the conductor called out, "Young People's Home," Salmonella began to weep.

"I'm not going."

Moldenke took her by the hand and pulled her into the aisle. "This is our stop. We're getting off."

She stiffened her body. "No!"

"Yes!" Moldenke dragged her up the aisle and down three steps to the pavement. On each step she banged her knees. By the time Moldenke had pulled to the Home's gate, streaks of blood ran down her legs and her kneecaps were shredded.

There was a Sister of Comfort at a sentry post. "Just the one, sir?"

"Yes. Abandoned by her father. I can't look after her."

"He could. But he won't, is the truth."

"What's your name, dear?"

Salmonella folded her arms and pouted. "Look at him. He needs my help. He can barely take care of himself. It's crazy to put me in here. He's as stupid as I thought he was when I met him."

"She calls herself Salmonella," Moldenke said. "She's about fourteen, fifteen. No one really knows—even her father."

"You can leave her with me," the Sister said. "We'll get those street clothes off, clean her up, and turn her loose on the commons."

"Thank you, ma'am," he said. "Just to clear something up, do the jellies in there have deformant?"

"All weapons are allowed."

"Guns?"

"Yes, guns. Knives, too. Anything, really. That's part of what we try to drill into these young people, that pure freedom is just that: pure. Once we're completely free in body and soul, we have no need of aggression. Everyone is safe, especially if they are armed. It keeps things in balance. It's the way freedom is arrived at."

Moldenke asked if there were any medical facilities on the grounds.

"A few of the kids know first aid," the Sister said. "Most of the wounds we have in here are not life-threatening. They usually survive."

Salmonella scowled at Moldenke.

"Sorry, girl...I'll try to find your father."

As Moldenke backed away from the gate, he saw Salmonella kick the Sister in the shin. In turn, the Sister slapped Salmonella with the back of her hand and pulled her up the path by the hair.

A comic book has nearly killed Brainerd Franklin, who didn't read but ate it. The laughter wasn't responsible for the damage, but part of the metal binding was. Wire staples found in the valuable jelly's stomach and intestinal tract were cause of his nearly fatal bleeding. A gardener had seen him floating in his swimming pool and munching on the comic only hours before his collapse.

Moldenke went down to the Free People's Bar, the only bitters bar operating on the west side. He found Udo there, who had been drinking bitters most of the afternoon.

"Where's my daughter, Moldenke? I want her back."

"She's in the Home. I left her there about a month ago."

"Tell me you didn't diddle her?"

"No, I took care of her. That's all."

"If I ever find out you did diddled her, I'll have your nuts for breakfast."

"It didn't happen."

"You understand why I wonder. She's mature for her age. Most of these freeborn girls are like that. They mate pretty young."

"If I mate at all, it will be with an older female. I couldn't attract anyone else. Look at me."

Udo had a quick look at Moldenke head to toe. "I'll take your word for it until I hear different. I guess I'll go over to the Home and get her."

"Whatever you want, Udo."

The next morning, with his courage up, Udo drove his motor to the curb in front of the Home. The sun ogled. Asphalt in the drive bubbled as he walked toward the mudstone entry gate where a Sister stood watch. Her blue uniform shimmered in the sunlight. She was eating a green apple.

"Good afternoon to you, Sister. I've come to get Salmonella. She was brought in by a man named Moldenke, oh, a few weeks ago. He's usually in uniform, wears boots. Has a scruffy little beard, rotten teeth. Sometimes smells bad."

The Sister ventured up to the heavy wooden doors that led onto the commons and opened them with a thrust of her shoulder. Udo saw the lush greenery inside: the orchard, the fields, and gardens. He saw the pig pens and chicken coops, the goat herd, the milking shed, all the things needed to sustain a body living the simple life. It was almost a shame, he thought, to take her out. Shaking his head and wishing the best for his daughter, he got into his motor and returned to the bar for another shot of bitters.

Salmonella, meanwhile, was busy squeezing apples with a press and selling the juice to other free youth by the cup.

"Your father is here to get you," the Sister said.

Salmonella stopped pressing for a moment. "I'm going to have an apple orchard of my own someday. Look, I've saved some seeds." She showed the Sister a little cloth sack full of apple seeds.

"That's nice, Salmonella." The Sister smiled as best she could. "Your father, he's waiting for you."

"He's not a fit father."

"Shall I tell him you'd rather stay here?"

"No, I'll give him one more chance."

The Sister looked at all the thirsty, anxious young people waiting in line for apple juice and stepped back. "I'll tell him you'll be along in a few minutes."

After two bitters, Udo thought that though the commons looked lush and the children were free of supervision, it didn't mean that Salmonella was better off there than on the outside, with a father. Not the father he had been, but the father he promised himself he would be. And all that freedom of will could mold her into something unmanageable altogether. Now his mind was changed.

Stiffened with bitters, Udo drove back to the Home in time to see the Sister escort Salmonella toward the entry gate. "Look, there he is. Your father," she said.

Udo tugged on the pull-crank that operated the side door of the motor and the Sister ushered Salmonella up the steps.

"Thank you, Sister," Udo said.

Salmonella sat just behind him. She was angry enough that he could feel her heat on the back of his neck. "I might kill you someday, Daddy, if you don't treat me better."

"I'm going to be nice to you from now on. You're my daughter."

"Where's my mother?"

"I've already told you a hundred times. They sent her back to Bunkerville. I haven't seen her since the day after the day you were born."

Salmonella shook her head and pointed a finger. "I don't believe you."

Udo made a fist. "Go back to your nook."

Salmonella had no wish to be slapped again. She went to her nook and lay on the cot.

Udo set the finder for Bunkerville and the motor responded with a sudden lurch, then entered the flow of vehicles on Arden Boulevard. In the rearview he saw the Sister waving.

Bunkerville radio last night issued a warning to free Altobelloans that anyone swimming in the Old Reactor pond risks exposure to radio poison, possibly a fatal dose. The report noted further that jellyheads—who have been swimming and bathing in the pond for a hundred years, long before the liberation—never exhibit signs of poisoning. It seems that over time jellies living near the Old Reactor have developed a resistance to the fatal malady.

Scientist Zanzetti and his assistants returned from Altobello with vials of the suspect water for study. In a public statement today the scientist said, "Even if you've been deformed, stay out of that water. It's heavy and it's dangerous. One swim, two swims, maybe three, and you'd be all right. More than that and death will follow as sure as I'm standing here on these two feet."

Unfortunately for many, the radio signal from Bunkerville, weakened by a little-understood effect of the full moon, never reached Altobello. The severely and moderately deformed continued swimming daily. In the dull, routine atmosphere that freedom brought them, along with shame of deformation, swimming was one of their greatest pleasures. They gladly took the risk.

After ten or more explosive angry-bowel incidents, Moldenke decided to have his uniform boiled. Getting a new one was a long, bureaucratic process that could take a year or more. Cleaning and sanitizing the pants, socks, and boots wasn't all that troublesome. He would take them to Myron's Boiling Service. Myron was an old Bunkerville friend who had once said to Moldenke, "Did you know that boiling a shoe for thirteen minutes will kill all fungi?" Myron claimed he could boil anything. The only problem was that his boilery was way out on Steaming Springs Road, not far from the Old Reactor. There were no streetcar tracks running out that far. It would be another long walk.

By the time Moldenke got to Steaming Springs Road, hoping all the while that Myron would still be open, his ankles ached terribly, yet he had a half mile to go. He could see the dome of the Old Reactor. The night was bright and there were moon shadows all around him. The dome's pitted surface could have been mistaken for the moon itself.

Myron's boiling business depended on the periodic, if random, cooling and boiling of the Springs. They were as likely to boil at night as any other time winter or summer. If they were boiling now, Myron would not be closed. He would be there with bitters in the cabinet, a fire in the stove, and Juleps to smoke.

As Moldenke walked on, the shadows playing in and out of the crepe myrtles than lined the road gave him the willies. A jellyhead gone critical could be lurking among them, planning to rush at him with a can of deformant. He thought the best strategy was to look straight ahead, to walk tall and purposefully, showing that he had a clear destination in mind. If a predator were stalking him, Moldenke didn't want to give the impression he was lost or disabled or otherwise vulnerable.

The mineral-rich steam rising from the little ditch that ran alongside the road indicated that the Springs were ready to boil, a strong sign that Myron might be open and in business. As Moldenke recalled, he was an affable sort and likable company. While the pants, shoes, and socks boiled he would probably sit with Moldenke in the kitchen drinking bitters and swapping stories about their lives in Bunkerville before they were set free.

Myron had been an art typist. On Saturdays and Sundays he could be found at a portable table in the Park at his Remington typewriter, pecking out the most intricate landscapes and portraits with letters, numbers, and diacritical marks. Strollers in the Park stopped to watch him. A small crowd often gathered, some to have Myron type their likeness for a thousand or two. Moldenke was often among the crowd and had two of Myron's works hanging in the hall at his aunt's house on Esplanade. His favorite was the head of Bunkerville mayor, Felix Grendon, whose features were etched perfectly in the artful strokes of Myron's Remington.

Then, one Sunday, Myron's table was not there. Strollers stopped, waited a while, and moved on. It was unusual, but then there was a chill in the air and a mist. Perhaps Myron, worried his machine would rust and the ink run, stayed home. It wasn't a serious concern until weeks went by without Myron's arriving with his machine in its case and the folding table and stool under his arm. Curious, Moldenke went to the Bunkerville Records Office and looked up the names of recent offenders sent to Altobello. Myron was there, detained three weeks and sent to the free city on two charges: selling private art in a public park and boiling jellyhead clothing.

The boiling service idea had come to Myron when he read in the *City Moon* that hundreds of pounds of gel-soiled clothing was either going to the dump or being burned in back yard fires. Jellies had been increasing in dramatic numbers and so were jelly killings, which more than likely ended in a well-aimed discharge of gel. Boiling, he knew, would neutralize the odor and restore the clothes and footwear to usability. He opened a small operation in his basement, but a shortage of wood to fuel enough fire to boil the water in his kettles threatened to close it quickly.

The facility at Steaming Springs came into Myron's possession when, out for a walk, he found the place abandoned. Apparently the it had ceased to boil after a hundred years of geothermal activity and the former boiling service had to close its doors.

Myron lived in a small house on the property, where he continued to pursue his art typing. Rather than haul his table and machine all the way into central Altobello, he simply carried his work in a portfolio and gave them away on the streets. That way he had nothing but grateful customers. He followed this routine every Sunday for months, then awoke one day to see steam rising again from the Springs. That night they were at full boil. The boilery was in business again.

When Moldenke arrived there and stood over the Springs, he looked down on an appalling scene: Myron's body floated atop the boiling water while a ring of jellyheads stood around the pool laughing. "He looks like a dead fish," one of them said. The naked body pinwheeled in the boiling, swirling current, its flesh bright red and split open in places.

One of the jellyheads spotted Moldenke and shouted, "Let's boil that guy, too." Three or four of them climbed toward him.

Exhausted as he was, Moldenke saw no other option but to run, and he did, as far as his sore ankles and breath would let him, dodging in and out of the crepe myrtles and eventually losing the two sluggish jellyheads trotting behind him. He was close enough to the byway to hear the rumble of speeding motors. He waved at passing vehicles, hoping one would stop and take him to the public bath near the Tunney.

Twenty or thirty went by. To make things worse, a hot, dry wind began with the first light of dawn. Moldenke remembered reading in a brochure that in some years Altobello was visited by an incessant wind, winter and summer, cold and hot that drove the early freemen half mad.

With his back to the traffic, Moldenke held out a thumb hoping that someone would see that he was far too weary and weak to do them any harm and offer him a lift. He heard one of the motors gearing down for a stop and turned to see Udo's motor pulling onto the shoulder of the pavement.

"Get in, Moldenke," Udo said, turning the crank that opened the door.

Moldenke got in and sat in the front passenger seat. "This is quite a coincidence, isn't it? Hundreds of motors going along the byway and there you are to pick me up."

"The roots of coincidence run deeper than we think, Moldenke. Our meeting in Point Blast, was that a coincidence?"

"I don't see any other explanation."

"Suit yourself. Be an idiot…What are you doing out here anyway?"

"Visiting a friend of mine at the boiler. Some jellies boiled him in the springs, then they were after me, chasing me. It's lucky you came by. I'm exhausted. I want to get a bath, some food, and back to the Tunney for sleep."

"I'll take you there, but luck had nothing to do with it."

"All right. Drop me off at the public bath. I'll walk the rest of the way."

"Will do."

When Udo accelerated in a final push toward Altobello, a spume of black foam shot from the motor's bleeder pipe. Udo saw it in the rear-view. "Bad break," he said. "The steamer is hot. We'll have to stop for the night. It'll take till dawn for it to cool down."

Udo angled the motor into the Black Hole Motel lot and turned off the engine. "We'll stay here tonight and have a shower."

Salmonella jumped out of her nook and clapped her hands. "Goody! Goody!" She put on a pair of rubber flip flops.

Udo said, "They tell me the workers at the Old Reactor used to stay here, so they have the best showers. Artesian well. Cold and clean."

Salmonella hurried to the lobby, stepping on hot asphalt most of the way. The bottoms of her flip-flops were coated with it. Udo and Moldenke followed, soft stepping over the asphalt. In the lobby, a fluff-haired desk clerk asked Udo, "You here for Coward's Day?"

Moldenke lit a Julep. "Is it Coward's Day already?"

"It sure is and we're almost full. Got one room left. Fifteen. It ain't the best one."

Udo showed his pass card and signed the register. "You *do* still have cold showers."

"Sometimes, if the pump's working. My husband, he got sent back to Bunkerville. I don't know how to fix nothing. It's room fourteen. Fifteen, I mean. Key's on that peg up there."

"I don't see any other motors in the lot," Moldenke said. "And you have only one vacancy?"

"Jelly families around here, they always come in on foot for Coward's Day. Heck, I can't stop 'em. You want the room or not?"

"Yes, we want a room," Salmonella huffed. "We stopped here, didn't we? Don't be so stupid."

"Excuse my daughter," Udo said. "She's been a mean young turd since I got her out of the Home. I'm going to slap her silly if she doesn't stop."

Salmonella snatched the key from the peg, ran toward the row of numbered rooms, and tried the key in fifteen. It fit, but was stubborn in the lock, refusing to turn. Eventually, after dozens of tries, the door opened to a burst of stale air. An ugly tableau presented itself. On the floor, beneath a hole in the ceiling, was a mound of rotting gel sacks with cockroaches roaming over it.

"This is bad," Salmonella said. We can't stay in here. Those things smell terrible." She put her hands on her hips. "And I'm hot. I want a shower."

"She said fifteen, didn't she?" Moldenke asked. "Maybe she meant fourteen. Let's try the key in fourteen."

The key did fit fourteen. The door opened to a musty but clean room with a shower stall and an electric light on the ceiling. There were folding cots leaning against the wall and a splintery dresser made of pine. Moldenke opened a drawer. Inside was a copy of the *Treatise* and several folding paper fans. He picked the *Treatise* up for a moment, looked at the fading cover, and put it back. He gave fans to Salmonella and Udo and took one himself. It was baking hot in the room. Opening the window only let in a blistering wind.

"I'm first in the shower!" Salmonella shrieked. She ducked into the stall and closed the oilcloth curtain.

Moldenke said, "I've been tied in such a knot the past few days that I haven't eaten anything. I'm hungry."

Udo unfolded a cot and lay down. "There's some kerd cakes in the motor. Go out and get them."

On the way to the motor, Moldenke passed an out-of-use swimming pool half full of water, a relic of the Black Hole's heyday, when the Old Reactor was under construction. Though the sun blinded him, he could shade his eyes with his hand and see two dead jellies floating in the pool's warm water. Their ear valves had been snipped off. Rats entered and exited holes in their bloated abdomens and gel from the leaking sacks streamed into the water and discolored it. Moldenke stepped away quickly.

After gathering up a few dried cakes of kerd and a couple of salted mud fish from the motor, Moldenke stopped at the motel office on the way to the room. He wanted to tell the clerk about the jellies in the pool. Perhaps she didn't know. But the blinds were drawn and his knock was not answered.

When he got back to the room, Salmonella had finished showering and was sitting on a cot in her petticoat, fanning herself. "Damn, it's hot in here."

Udo sang in the shower, "Hang out yer laundry on the Siegfried line...dad a da, dad a da."

"I saw two dead jellies in the pool," Moldenke said. "Someone got to them before your daddy did."

"Don't tell him. He'll get excited."

Moldenke offered a cake of kerd to Salmonella. "This is all we have, except for a couple of mud fish."

"No green soda?"

"Sorry, no."

"I want green soda!"

"Please, for your own good, stop shouting. We don't want any trouble. In the morning we'll stop at the first Saposcat's we see."

"You promise?"

"I promise."

"I like you better than Daddy. He's mean."

"He's your father. That's all there is to it."

"I'd like to kill him. I think I will."

"To be honest, there's no law here that says you can't. Back in Bunkerville, you'd be exploded for doing it."

Udo finished showering and it was Moldenke's turn. He took off his filthy clothes and entered the stall. Aside from being cold, what weak flow of water came from the shower head smelled of sulfur but was good enough to rinse off the patina of sweat and body dander that crusted him. Now, until he could get his dirty uniform boiled, it was a matter of putting it on an almost clean body.

He, Salmonella, and Udo settled into their cots. Moldenke wanted to keep the ceiling light on for a while so he could read parts of the *Treatise* to put himself to sleep.

Udo grunted then turned over. "I don't care. I feel sick."

Salmonella was wide awake. "Read to me. I can't sleep."

Moldenke read and partly paraphrased as he went along: "This is a chapter about the cries of animals...'The angry tones of wild beasts can cause an awful sensation. It might seem that these modulations of sounds are not arbitrary but are related to the things they represent. But the main thing is, they make themselves understood.'"

Salmonella sat up. "So that means when a dog barks, other dogs know what that means. I've heard of dogs. They don't have any in Altobello. Or if a bird sings, other birds understand."

"Right. I think that's what it means."

By this time Udo was snoring loudly. His throat gurgled, his nostrils whistled with every breath. Sometimes the breathing stopped altogether for as long as a minute.

"Maybe he'll die in his sleep," Salmonella said.

"Never mind that," Moldenke said. "Let me finish reading this and I'll turn out the light...So, Burke says that our language is not so clear as the language of animals. Yet the modifications of sound in our language could be what's sublime about it, as opposed to theirs, which is merely beautiful, because our language is almost infinite, which cannot be said of theirs."

Now Salmonella was asleep and Moldenke's lids were heavy. He closed the *Treatise* and lay his weary head back against the canvas cot and fell quickly to sleep.

In the morning, when he awoke, Udo was oiling and cleaning his niner. Salmonella still slept.

"You see any jellies out there, Moldenke?"

"No, none. They must be napping."

"I don't feel good. I'm not in the mood anyway. Let's get on the road. The steamer's cool by now. You drive."

Moldenke felt refreshed after a good enough sleep. "I'll go to the office and check us out."

Udo handed Moldenke a time worn card with flayed edges. "What kind of card do you have? You're new here. It might not cover this kind of luxury. Take mine."

Moldenke walked over to the Black Hole office. The clerk was reading Burke's *Treatise* and drinking from a mug of tea. "You people checking out?"

"We will be, yes. But I wanted to let you know, you've got two jellies dead in the old pool."

The clerk lit a Julep and closed her book. "Jellies in the pool?"

"Two, with cut off valves."

"Well, these are Cowards' Days you know. There's a lot of excitement. Jellies get shot. We find bodies all the time."

Moldenke placed Udo's pass card on the counter. "All right, then. I won't worry about it. I'll just go back to the room and we'll get going."

The clerk looked at the card suspiciously. "This is an old one." She sniffed it.

"It belongs to my travel companion. I'm sure it's a good card. He's been here a long time."

She gave the card back to Moldenke. "Happy motoring."

Udo was in a foul mood when Moldenke returned to number fourteen. "I feel like death eating a cracker," he said, "I think that little witch there poisoned me."

Salmonella yawned. "I'm starving. Let's go now."

Udo raised his fist at her. "Shut up before I come over there and kick you hard. Can't you see I'm sick?"

"Let's go then," Moldenke said. "He hoped Udo wouldn't see the jellies in the pool as they walked to the motor and did his best to distract him by blathering on about the *Treatise*. "Really, Udo, who cares about the sublime and the beautiful? We have other things to think about, more urgent things. It's a shame that's the only book we can get here. There was a time when I read books. I was more alert. I could focus on things. Now I can't." Udo never saw the jellies, bent over as he was by stomach cramps.

"I did *not* poison him," Salmonella said. "That gun oil got him sick."

Udo burbled and seemed ready to upchuck.

The motor started up on the first crank. Moldenke let it run in place until he was sure there was no spume coming from the bleeder pipe then pulled onto the Byway and set the finder for Saposcat's.

Udo slumped in the passenger's seat, favoring his stomach and complaining now of a headache. Salmonella stood behind Moldenke as he drove. She spit on her finger and stuck it into his ear. "Wet Willie!"

"Stop that."

"Hurry up. Drive fast."

She gave him another Wet Willie.

"Stop that, please."

Saposcat's was crowded. They were offering a Coward's Day breakfast special of mud fish and kerd. Udo sat on one side of a booth, Salmonella and Moldenke on the other. Most of the diners wore yellow Coward's Day regalia.

The scrape of leg flesh signaled the approach of the waitress. "Morning. You all here for Cowards' Day?"

"No, we're not," Moldenke said. "We're headed for the west side."

"You ought to stay. It's something to see, I'll tell you."

"We're in a hurry."

"Okay, what'll it be?"

Salmonella said, "Give me the special, with green soda."

"Sorry, girl, if you're not here for Coward's Days, you can't have the special. You can get something else if you want."

"That's pretty stupid. Give me the kerd then."

"We're out of kerd."

"Okay, the mud fish and green soda. This is all pretty stupid."

"Mud fish and soda. That we got. You, sir?"

Udo wanted only a cup of tea and a bowl of meal.

Moldenke ordered the same, telling the waitress, "I don't digest things very well. Angry bowel."

"Well, sir. There's a privy out back in case."

The waitress returned to the kitchen.

It seemed that the act of mentioning his bowel triggered a strong contraction in Moldenke's gut. "I'm going out back." He slid from the booth and headed for the door. A few strides in that direction and he stepped into a hole in the floor, scraping his shin on the splintered wood. Salmonella helped him out of the hole.

"You okay?"

Some of the Coward's Days enthusiasts laughed.

The waitress came to help. "Sorry, it's a rotten spot that fell through."

The fry cook rushed out of the kitchen wearing a home-made cloth veil. "What's going on here? Is there trouble?"

Moldenke was almost in tears. "Why don't you put up a *sign*?"

The fry cook raised his fist and took an angry step forward, but the waitress blocked his way. She massaged his shoulder and neck to calm him then said to Moldenke, "We're sorry.

It would be nice to have a sign. That spot's been fixed but it just rots again."

The fry cook, becalmed now, said, "You're lucky, fella. When we opened this morning, some old jelly broke her leg in that hole. I heard it snap like a twig."

The crowd twittered and giggled.

Moldenke raised his trouser leg to examine the cut on his ankle. It was more of a gouge than a clean cut, and the bleeding was slight. He continued on to the privy out back and discovered three privies instead: one for males, one for females, and one for jellyheads. He went first into the privy for males, found the commode ringed with drying feces, then tried the female privy. When he opened the door, there sat the waitress, squinting to read the *Treatise* in dim light. She wasn't startled or offended and said, "Angry bladder."

"Please excuse me. I didn't know anyone was in here. You were just inside a moment ago."

"Don't worry, it happens all the time. That's my sister. We look alike. Not twins, but we look alike."

"Oh."

"I work in the kitchen if I'm not out here taking care of business."

"Well, again, my apologies."

"Use the one for jellyheads. It's the best."

"All right, thanks."

Moldenke found the jellyhead privy in a clean condition, with only a slight odor and no sign of the *Treatise*. There was a bucket of water on the ground and a selection of old socks for wiping hanging from nails in the wall.

In that setting, relaxed, Moldenke had a strong and productive bowel movement before wiping with a sock that he rinsed it in the sink and hung on a nail. He limped back to the booth, passing close to the kitchen, where he saw the fry cook drop an unlit kitchen match into deep fat. After float-ing a moment, the match burst into flame. "She's ready to fry stuff," he said.

Moldenke said to Udo, "If you have to take a leak or any-thing, use the jellyhead privy. It's the best one out there."

"Thanks for the tip."

Moldenke's ankle throbbed. "Why couldn't they fix that hole? If there was law here, I'd sue them for all they're worth. You just get some wood and you fix the hole."

"No carpenters," Udo said. "And hardly any wood. If you want to fix the floor, you have to rip wood from some other part of the building. That's the way it is here."

"I didn't see that in the brochures."

"Pure freedom means no money, no law, nothing. Think about it."

"We pay nothing for our rooms," Moldenke said, light-ing a Julep, "or the food. We've got streetcars and pass cards. Good bear claws in the Old Quarter. Passable sausages at Smiley's Meats, too. It's not so bad. I'm getting used to it."

The waitress set the food on the table. "There's your orders."

Salmonella asked, "Why is that stupid cook wearing a veil. Is he deformed?"

The waitress whispered, "Yeah, but not from deformant. A jellyhead mother threw her baby through that kitchen window over there. It landed in the fryer and splashed him with hot oil, mostly in the face. People don't like looking at him while they're eating."

Salmonella asked, "Did the little jelly get fried?"

"It did, black as a cinder."

The fry cook called out, "Order up!"

"Why do they kill their babies?" Salmonella asked.

Moldenke shrugged. "Why do they cut off heads and leave them at Saposcat's?"

"Zanzetti'll figure it out," Udo said. "It's got something to do with their gel sacks."

The food was served by the woman Moldenke had seen in the privy. "Hi, there," she said to him. "I saw you outside. It's my sister's turn now. She's got a bad stomach."

Moldenke blushed. "I apologize again for barging in on you."

"It's nothing. Here, enjoy your food."

Salmonella picked up a mud fish whole and bit into it above the fin, the crispiest part, and complained it was cold.

Udo said, "Eat it anyway. There's a storm coming. We're not staying any longer than we have to."

Moldenke ate his meal rapidly and drank his tea with a single lift of the cup, then waved his pass card. "This one's on me. Thanks for the ride."

The waitress brought the bill and checked pass cards. "Where you three headed?"

"The west side."

"Big change in the weather. Snowstorm coming, you know? Drive careful."

Dear Moldenke.

You'll be glad to know that I am leading a strike of the Bunkerville garbage men. Some pretty unsanitary conditions have begun to arise as the result of the work halt. Little boys are running barefoot through great steaming mounds of trash and refuse, their childish cheerfulness undimmed by the fact that with every passing day another twenty thousand tons of garbage is added to the heaps already decomposing in the hot sun. Talk of the plague is on every tongue.

The paper asked scientist Zanzetti about it and he said, "No one can say we weren't forewarned. It's only a matter of time until Bunkerville is completely liberated. This strike is an early sign."

You see, we're eventually going to liberate this city one strike at a time. When you get back, everything will be different. No one can go up to the striking garbage men with their crudely lettered "Stink City" placards and their brutish oaths and say, "I'm very sorry but somebody has to pick up the garbage and on this particular turn of the wheel it looks like you." No one has the charisma needed for a job like that. We will not lose this battle.

Ozzie

Despite the sudden drop in temperature and the three-inch accumulation of snow on the ground, Altobello's outskirts, mostly scrublands, were thronged with jellyheads celebrating Cowards' Days. Some had even spilled out onto the byway, causing a hazard for passing motors. Most drivers made an effort to avoid hitting them, uncontrollably sliding this way and that in the process. Other drivers made no such effort and ran them over, leaving the snow gooey with gel and blood.

Salmonella shouted, "Look, they're making snow angels. Don't run over them! Let them have their fun."

Moldenke maneuvered the motor around them.

"I don't know what they're celebrating, or why they call it Cowards' Days," Udo said. "In jellyhead history, is there some kind of famous coward?"

Moldenke said, "Who knows? Maybe cowards were honored for ending a war by giving up. Did the jellyheads ever have a war? I can't remember."

"They're awful aggressive with deformant," Udo said.

Moldenke burped several times then angled into a little pullout with a picnic table and a privy for public use. "My bowel, we'll have to stop."

There was another motor there, balanced precariously with a flimsy axle jack straining under the load. One of the side tires had been removed and lay flat on the ground.

Salmonella frowned. "Hurry up. I don't like this place."

Udo said, "I count six jellies sitting in that motor. One of them has a baby and it's crying. Can't you hear it? Why aren't they changing the tire?"

"Pull out," Salmonella shouted. "Drive right through. Get back on the highway. This looks bad. We shouldn't stop."

Udo said, "Shut up!"

"Don't blame me if there's trouble," Salmonella said. "Those are bad jellies."

"They look decent enough to me," Moldenke said. "Like a family." He walked to the privy without incident, stopping to scoop a handful of snow for wiping. He knew there would be no paper. The jellies watched him enter and waited quietly until he came out.

Udo checked to see that his niner was loaded. If one of them made a move toward Moldenke or a threatening gesture, he would aim to kill. He had an eye on the privy and the jellies too. Salmonella sat at one of the windows watching. When the privy door opened and Moldenke stepped out, one of the jellies leaped from the back door of the crowded motor with a baby. "Please change that tire. We don't know how."

Udo snarled and shouted out the window, "They're trying to trick you. Don't look them in the eye."

Moldenke said, "No, I think they really need help. I'll change the tire."

"You're stupid, Moldenke," Salmonella said.

Moldenke set about changing the tire in the biting cold, his fingers quickly numbed. The jelly with the half-frozen baby stood over him, cradling it. "Hurry up, you. My baby's cold and I've got sack rot. I'll be dead in a week."

Moldenke was aggravated by her tone and no longer sympathetic. "Take the baby inside the motor. I'm sorry about the rot, but don't stand out here watching me."

"My husband's got bad sacks too."

"I'm doubly sorry then. I'll change the tire. Don't watch me."

The jellyhead mother didn't seem to understand what Moldenke was saying, as if he were speaking a foreign language. The baby licked the drips from one of her valves. The sight and the smell of it disgusted Moldenke.

The mother backed away, not far, and watched from a different vantage.

When the tire was mounted, Moldenke jacked down the vehicle, tightened the lug nuts, tapped the hubcap on, and put the tire tool, the jack, and the flat tire in the rear storage trunk.

"There you go. Glad to help out jellies in trouble. Too bad about the sack rot. It's a sad thing, I guess."

Moldenke climbed back into the motor. Udo, sitting in the driver's seat, said, "I feel better. I'll drive," then stepped on the accelerator. As the machine rolled forward slowly, the jellyhead mother threw her baby under the rear wheels. The bump, then the crush of bones, could be heard and felt inside the motor.

Moldenke stood and looked back. "Should we stop?" He put his head out of a side window to get a better look at what had happened.

Two male jellies ran behind with cans of deformant.

Udo opened a red-handled petcock on the dash, juicing up the flow of heavy water and the motor rolled faster, but only until it reached a small grade leading back to the Byway, where it stalled long enough for several of the deformant-wielding jellies to catch up.

Udo reached over to pull Moldenke in. "Get back in here!" It was moments too late. One of the jellies had already squirted him on the side of the head. His ear foamed and burned like fire. The hand he had put up to deflect the spray was burned and blistering.

"I *told* you, stupid," Salmonella said.

"I'm learning to listen, girl. I'm learning to listen."

Udo drove the motor along Arden in a drizzle. The snow had stopped, the air had warmed, and gutters were running with dirty slush. Salmonella, for reasons unknown, thought about her mother. She grew restless and asked Udo, "Where is my mother?"

"Stop playing that old tune, girl. I'm blue in the face from telling you your mother went back to Bunkerville."

By this time Moldenke had become convinced that Salmonella, as a freeborn, had no capacity for familial feelings and he was surprised to see her showing such curiosity about her mother.

"I want to know how old I am," Salmonella said.

"A mother would probably know," Moldenke said.

Udo's pale face pinked. "I've told you a hundred times, you're about sixteen or seventeen."

"Fifteen, maybe? Or eighteen?"

"It's possible. I don't remember." Udo fingered his niner. "She needs to go back to the Home. Let's take her to the Home."

Moldenke wondered if the Home was open all night.

"Please don't take me there again." Salmonella pretended to snuffle.

Moldenke looked away. It was not his business.

"It's a good place," Udo said, "better than out here where freedom stinks. In there, it's educational. You're going in. It will be better for you. Listen to your daddy."

Moldenke agreed, "Maybe he's right. The Home would be the best place for you now."

Udo brightened with an idea. "Do me a favor, Moldenke. Put her up in your room for the night and take her to the Home tomorrow. So we don't kill one another."

Tired as he was, with his ear throbbing and hot to the touch, Moldenke took the offer. He had had enough squabbling for the day and needed rest.

Salmonella said, "Moldenke, there's something coming out of your ear." A waxy brown liquid had begun to run from the canal and the rest of the ear showed small white-tipped pustules. "I'll stay with you. You need help."

"Your call, Moldenke," Udo said.

Moldenke thought Salmonella's company for the night could prove to be an asset. She would distract him from his deformity, if nothing else. Aerosol deformant's effects were unpredictable. Even a small amount could lead to significant changes in facial structure, with blistering, seeping, and intermittent bleeding.

"All right," Moldenke said. "I get the cot, you get the chair."

Salmonella squared her shoulders. "I'll be your nurse. You do what I say. You'll get better."

"All right."

"But don't take me to the Home."

Udo parked the motor around the corner from the Tunney Arms while Salmonella packed a few things from her nook into a leather bag.

Udo said, "Get her to the Home as quick as you can. You understand me, Moldenke?"

"Sure. We'll take the streetcar tomorrow if they're running."

"Don't you be diddling her, you hear?"

"I hear. That's not going to be a problem."

The concierge, asleep in a wooden chair in her little receiving room, woke up when Moldenke and Salmonella entered the foyer. She stood at her Dutch door yawning. "Who is that girl? One room, one person. That's the way we do it."

"It's just for the night. She'll be going to the Home tomorrow. No real mother, no real father."

Salmonella produced a tear. "I'm an orphan. Let me stay. This poor man needs help. Look at his ear."

The concierge put on her bifocals and looked at Moldenke's ear. "You've gotten yourself deformed, haven't you?"

"It was a light dose," Moldenke said, and hoped. "It may resolve itself. Who knows?"

"Here, I have something." The concierge went into an adjacent room, a kitchenette, and returned with a small bottle labeled *Barrel Honey Concentrate*. "It's anti-deformant from Zanzetti Labs. Try it. Rub it in."

Moldenke could see beyond the kitchenette, through a slightly opened door, a commode, and next to it, on the floor, a pre-liberation roll of tissue for wiping.

"Is that a wet commode, ma'am? You hardly ever see those."

"My husband built it for me after the liberation, before he went back to Bunkerville. There's a big rain barrel on the roof. That's what flushes it all into a lagoon he dug out back."

"That's really something," Moldenke said.

"It makes life a little better for me."

"I'm certain it does," Moldenke said. "I see a bathtub, too."

"It doesn't drain and can't be used."

"All right then. Thank you."

Moldenke had one more thing to ask the concierge. "Is there any mail for me? A friend is looking after my house in Bunkerville. He's promised to keep me posted about it."

She looked through a small stack of letters. "Yes, you did get one."

Moldenke opened the dirtied envelope and took a few minutes to read the letter.

> *Dear Moldenke,*
>
> *All is mostly well at the house on Esplanade except I think there might be termites in the door frames. The wood is crumbling. And some sort of animal, maybe a ground hog, has dug a deep hole in the back yard, which is convenient because the house toilet doesn't work at all and I use the hole as a latrine. Didn't you say something about maintenance money for this place? How do I get it? Does it come by mail?*
>
> *Hope you're doing well in Altobello. In so many ways, I wish I were there. But I see my job as staying and doing what I can to liberate Bunkerville. My aim is to have the place completely free when you return.*
>
> *Your friend,*
> *Ozzie*

Moldenke gave the concierge the awkward little salute he always gave when he felt uneasy. "All right, thank you. Good night."

Salmonella grasped Moldenke's hand and led him up the stairs and into his room, where a dim bulb hung from the ceiling by an electric wire, not giving enough light to get a good look at the damages to his ear and the flesh around it.

He had to rely on Salmonella's sharp young eyes to describe it to him as he lay on the cot.

"It's red and purple and leaking brown stuff." She applied barrel honey concentrate to the ear. "We don't want it to get any worse. This might help."

The heaviness of the ear tilted Moldenke's head sideward and downward. His swollen hand now lay beside him on the cot without sensation. "Put some on that ankle gouge, too. It's festering."

Salmonella dipped a finger into the honey and gently spread it over the wound. "Why do you want to put me in the Home? You need somebody to take care of you. I can do that."

Moldenke's lids sank over his eyes. "We'll see what to-morrow brings."

The morning brought a raucous noise from the street. Moldenke went to the window. There were a few hundred jellyheads marching along Arden Boulevard tooting kazoos. They held no banners, carried no flags, sang no songs, and shouted no epithets or slogans. He wondered what had got-ten them out at dawn to march that way without apparent cause or purpose. It wasn't even Cowards' Day, but the day after.

Salmonella joined him at the window. "Who are they? What are they marching for?"

"I don't know," Moldenke said. "It could be anything."

Salmonella scratched her head. "I'm hungry. Let's go to Saposcat's."

"All right. How does my ear look?"

"Pretty ugly."

The concierge stopped them on the way out.

"How's that ear today?"

Salmonella shook her head. "Bad."

"Did you rub it good with that honey?"

"Yes. It didn't help."

"Show me that ear. Let me see it."

"No time. I've got to get to the privy right away. I've got a condition."

"His bowels get angry," Salmonella said. "He potties in his pants all the time."

"Like Franklin, the famous golfer," Moldenke said. "We have the same problem."

"For goodness sake, go ahead and use my crapper."

"Thank you so much."

"Hurry up," Salmonella mumbled.

Moldenke entered the little toileting room and savored the look of the wet commode. He hadn't seen one since Bunkerville, and seldom then. It was clean and the porcelain gleamed, even in dull light. On a small wooden stool within his reach was a copy of Burke's *Treatise*. Although he was curious to read a bit of the well-worn copy, he didn't want to overstay his time on the commode. He sat down and relieved himself with exquisite pleasure, then carefully unrolled the paper, wound it thickly around his sore hand, and wiped himself, careful not to get fecal contaminant on the cracked, slightly bleeding palm. When he flushed, the water swirled with energy and quickly emptied the bowl. *"Really nice,"* he said to himself. *"Really nice setup."*

He wondered if perhaps the concierge might somehow be persuaded to give him toileting privileges when he needed them and began to consider what approach to take toward that end. What could he offer her? Everything in Altobello was technically free. Would she accept an exchange of janitorial services? But what could he do with his sore hand the way it was. He wouldn't be able to sweep or mop.

No, he decided to put it to her foursquare. He said, "What can I do in exchange for use of that commode? I never know when the need will strike. It could be in the middle of the night. I can't be running down to the public privy all the time. You seem like a kind woman. Please."

"When the rain water up there freezes, it doesn't work. And you'll need to find your own paper. They always have extra down at the privy. Just take some."

"All right, that's fair."

"And when the lagoon out back gets full, I expect you to help me cart it down to the ditch in buckets."

"Of course I will."

"Please don't tell the other guests you're using my commode. I'll have a line out here."

"I won't say a word."

Salmonella patted her stomach. "Let's go eat."

"Wait," Moldenke said. He asked the concierge, "Why were they marching out there this morning? Who were they?"

"The Cowards that weren't killed yesterday. They're headed home. I hear they stay out by the Old Reactor."

Moldenke shook his head and pulled on his chin beard. "They're an odd bunch, aren't they? No one understands their customs."

"You can say that again," she said. "Here's another letter for you."

Dear Moldenke,

You'd be happy with what I'm doing toward liberating Bunkerville. I've now organized the ice men. They've been on strike for three weeks. As a result I read in the paper that a check of available ice has revealed that sixty percent of it is contaminated with anything from insect parts and fish scales to mold, pieces of wood, paint flakes and human vomit. All of this because of my work for and dedication to freedom. I know you share my sentiments.

I've had no luck in getting access to your aunt's maintenance funds. But I won't dwell on that right now. Instead, I'll tell you, I've rented out a room to a jellyhead mason in exchange for repairing the crumbling wall on the north side. He is a nice sort, very quiet and reserved, but works hard. And the best part is he has a friend who knows a bit about plumbing. I'm thinking of renting another room to him on the same terms.

That cesspool forming in the yard is getting a lot of complaints from the few neighbors who haven't left for the countryside. There is a kind of mild, measured panic here as we anticipate the coming liberation.

Anyway, I hope is all well with you and that you can soon return to take up the cause again.

Ozzie

At Saposcat's, the breakfast special was meal with fried kerd. "Perfect," Moldenke told the waitress. "What could be better for my stomach? I'll have the special."

Salmonella's lips pruned. "Kerd I like. I'll vomit if I eat meal."

"There are other things," Moldenke said. "Get what you want. You're going to the Home today. Enjoy these few hours outside."

"I'll have the fried kerd, a plate of mud fish, and a bottle of green soda."

"Be back with that in a minute."

Salmonella pouted and kicked Moldenke's leg lightly. "You promise?"

"Promise what?"

"That you'll take me back to Bunkerville when you go. Maybe my mother's there. Maybe I'll find her."

"I'm not going to promise anything. I could be sent back to Bunkerville any day anyway. I'm indeterminate. If you were my ward we'd have to say goodbye then and you'd be all on your own."

"Is Bunkerville free? Is it liberated?"

"Not yet. You don't want to go there."

"Are there apple trees in Bunkerville with apples to pick?"

"I've never seen one."

"Have you ever eaten an apple?"

"I know all about them from pictures."

"Take me to Bunkerville. I'll grow the trees myself. Promise me right now you'll take me to Bunkerville."

"There are still laws there and police. For a free person like you, it would be a jail sentence."

"What's a jail?"

"You're locked up in a small room with metal doors."

"Why?"

"For killing someone, for example. Stealing, cheating, fraud, the list goes on and on."

"Oh. That's pretty stupid."

"They're not free yet," Moldenke said. "They're still trying to control things, to keep order or something. They don't want a chaotic situation."

Moldenke was served a bowl of meal and a side dish of kerd. He tucked right into the pasty mash with a spoon. Salmonella ate her mud fish from the head down—gills, bones, innards and fins. By the time she had finished, her gums were bleeding. She said, "Take me to the Home. I'm ready."

It was late in the evening when Moldenke and Salmonella arrived by streetcar at the Home. A lamp burned in a mud brick kiosk near the gate post. A Sister sat inside reading the *City Moon* and smoking a Julep.

Moldenke said, "All right, Salmonella. I wish you the best. Go on to the Sister."

Salmonella took one step down and turned. "Don't leave Altobello without me. We'll go to Bunkerville, and when I'm ready we'll mate, we'll have some children, and we'll grow apples."

The prospect of that happening seemed extremely remote to Moldenke, so he simply smiled and gave Salmonella an ambiguous nod. As the car pulled away, he watched her until she had explained things to the Sister and was headed toward the gate to the commons.

> *Dear Ozzie,*
>
> *To get the maintenance money, you must go to the First Bunkerville Bank and tell them you are the appointed custodian of the house. If they ask for documentation or proof of any kind, see my aunt's attorney. His name is McPhail and he has an office on Broad Street. It's only a few blocks up Esplanade. I will write him and tell him you are to be the tenant and the responsible party when it comes to maintenance. You say all is well, but the things you list are alarming. Please take care of them as soon as possible. I am deeply concerned.*
>
> *As far as taking up the cause, I'm not sure liberation is the best thing for Bunkerville. I'll postpone judgment on that.*
>
> *Your friend,*
> *Moldenke*

Moldenke, relieved that Salmonella was no longer around, had a yen for bear claw the next morning and caught the Arden car going to the Quarter. The car's windows were open to cool, pleasant breezes and the sun shone brightly. There were even a few blooming crepe myrtles along the route. Things seemed quite mild and relaxing until the car stopped at the entrance to the Quarter for the usual boarding and inspection. A guard got on the car and walked up and down the aisle looking suspiciously at the passengers. Sometimes he would stop and bend over until his face was inches from theirs. When he came to Moldenke's seat, he did just that. "Got yourself squirted, eh?"

"Yeah, it's not too bad, but it still stings and burns and itches sometimes."

"They tell me people are starting to swim in that pond out by the Old Reactor. They say the heavy water heals those deformations better than anything."

"All right. I might try that."

"I'll tell you, if I ever get deformed, look for me in that pond."

Sensing that the guard was not as gruff as he appeared, Moldenke said, "Say, can I ask you a question?"

"Of course, fire away."

"When you board the car and you stare at everyone, what exactly are you looking for?"

"Nothing, it's just for show. I enjoy doing it. I like people to remember what it was like before the liberation."

"I'm new here. I didn't know."

"People forget what it was like. So I developed this act and they let me do it. Everybody gets a kick out of it."

"Thanks for the information."

"You bet. Welcome to the Quarter."

Moldenke got off at the stop nearest Big Ernie's and saw a tobacconist's kiosk with a rusty Julep sign. "You're in luck," the tobacconist said. "We've got the cork-tipped in stock."

"Good. You can't get them over on the west side. I'll have two packs."

The tobacconist looked at Moldenke's pass card. "Sorry, only one at a time with this kind of card. You'll get a better card after a year."

"Give me one pack then."

Walking on, Moldenke sat on the steps of the Church of the Lark to have a smoke. His matches were soggy and wouldn't light easily. He had to strike them over and over just to get a hiss and a sputter. He began eyeing passersby for ones likely to have a match and chose a thin, anxious man he saw smoking the stub of a hand-made cigar.

Moldenke took a few steps toward the man. "Pardon me. Do you have a light?"

The man shivered a little, puffed on his cigar, and came toward Moldenke with a lit match. "Here you go." Moldenke could now see the other side of the man's face. One cheek and the right eye were deformed. Without lids, the eyeball protruded grotesquely. Some of the healed-over flesh of the face looked yellowed and waxen.

"Thank you." Moldenke inhaled deeply. It was the first Julep he'd had for a while.

They sat on the church steps. "I'm here on indefinite," the man said, "for stealing a duck from the park. What about you?"

"Defacing a grave. Also indefinite. I see you've been squirted."

"A little jellyhead son of a bitch in the Park."

Moldenke turned his head. "They squirted me too. I took some on the ear, as you can see, and a little on the hand. Was he naked and wearing a fancy cap?"

"Had a hell of donnicker, too. Slapped it with his knees when he was running at me."

"Don't worry. I took care of that little menace, if you know what I mean—a favor for Big Ernie over at the bear claw place. That same jelly deformed his daughter."

"I know Big Ernie. The body on that daughter is so very nice. I'd give anything to mate with her, but Big Ernie doesn't like me."

One of the Sisters burst out of the church with a broom and waved it wildly. "Get away from here, you bums."

"Hey," the man protested, "aren't you supposed to give us comfort?"

The Sister grimaced and placed a hand on her hip. "Go on, get moving."

Moldenke and the deformed man parted company, going separate ways amid the sidewalk crush.

The green light was on at Big Ernie's. A line extended out the front door. Moldenke took his place behind a young free woman reading Burke's *Treatise*. For a few minutes, as the line moved slowly forward, Moldenke looked over her shoulder and tried to read some of the text. With his weak eyesight it was impossible. "Excuse me," he said, "why is everyone reading that book?"

Without turning all the way, she said, "It's the only one you can get these days. They're old, falling apart, pre-liberation."

"Where can I get a one?"

"People throw them away. I found this one in a gutter on the west side."

"Thanks. I'll keep my eyes open."

Sorrel greeted Moldenke with a frown when he reached the counter. "What happened to your ear, Moldenke? It looks awful."

"Out on the Byway. Some jellyhead got me."

It was then that Moldenke saw how much Sorrel's face had improved. Much of the scarring had gone away. Her lips were fuller and a healthy red.

"You look better, Sorrel. Your face is healing. Are you treating it with something? Barrel honey maybe?"

"I've been bathing in the Old Reactor pool. Something in the water re-forms flesh and bone. Everybody's doing it. You should give it a try. I'll go with you. Come here at eight sharp tomorrow. Knock on the door. We're closed on Sunday."

"Very good. I'll be here."

"Where is that nasty little girl you had?"

"She's in the Home. I'm rid of her."

"Good. How many claws?"

"Give me four." He showed his card.

"Oops, sorry, you can get only two with that kind of card."

"Yeah, I forgot."

As he waited for the Arden car, Moldenke ate one of the warm bear claws, which settled well in his stomach. He would save the other one and offer it to the concierge when he got back to the Tunney. It would be a decent gesture and give him further leverage in maintaining his toilet privileges. He wrapped the waxed paper tightly around it, put it into his pocket, and boarded the car.

There were very few open seats, all of them in the rear, where jellyheads generally liked to sit. It was a Saturday afternoon and free men and women were taking advantage of the pleasant weather while it lasted. Hundreds had been out walking in the Quarter and were now going home. Having no choice, Moldenke sat with the jellyheads. Next to him was an elderly female with a small, bulging suitcase leaking blood at the seams. "Hi, there," the jellyhead said.

"Hello."

"I apologize for the stink. There's two heads in here, my husband's and my lazy son's. I'm taking them to Saposcat's. We lived out by the Old Reactor."

"Did you ever bathe in the pond?"

"When I was a kid, all the time. Then they wouldn't let us anymore, after the liberation. That water was good for us."

"I'm going to swim there tomorrow." He turned his head so that she could see the other side. "For this ear. Maybe it'll re-form."

"Maybe it will, but I wouldn't stay in that pond too long. What's good for us might be bad for a regular like you."

"Thanks for the warning."

She hefted the dripping suitcase. "Excuse me, but next stop is Saposcat's."

"Mine too," Moldenke said. He stood up to let the jellyhead pass, his ankle throbbing, his ear still sore and burning. The two got off together. Moldenke held her elbow as she went down the steps, helping to balance the heavy suitcase.

"Thank you so much," she said.

The two parted pays on the sidewalk—the jellyhead to leave the heads at Saposcat's, Moldenke to the Tunney for some rest.

When he got there, already tired with the day only half done, the concierge was bent over her commode cleaning the bowl with a long brush.

"I have a bear claw for you, from Big Ernie's in the Quarter," he told her.

"Oh, isn't that sweet. Thank you." She put away the brush and came to her little Dutch door, through which she could monitor any comings and goings in the foyer, the stairs, and the hallway. "I just love them."

"I'm going there tomorrow. I'll bring you another one. I have a date with Big Ernie's daughter. We're going out to soak in the Old Reactor pond. It might help this ear."

"That's nice. The water is wonderful and she's a fine girl. I know her and Big Ernie. Would you like to use the toilet before you go up to your room?"

Moldenke's bowel, while not angry, was anxious. Better now than later it was telling him.

"I suppose so, yes. Thanks."

The concierge opened the bottom half of her Dutch door and let him into her small apartment. He turned toward the little room with the commode and she followed him there, stepping on his heels once or twice on the way. When he tried to close the door, she stopped him. "Leave it open. I want to watch."

He'd been many times sitting hip to hip with strangers in public privies but never had anyone wanted to stand by and watch him empty his bowels. If that was the price he was going to have to pay now to have access to this sublime convenience, then he would pay it.

"Do you mind if I read a bit? It isn't going to come easily."

"That's fine. I'm just watching. Do what you would do."

Moldenke looked up at a boarded-over window above the bathtub. "Too bad about that," he said. "We could be getting some air in here."

"My husband did that when the liberation was happening. A lot of glass was getting broken."

Moldenke picked up Burke's *Treatise*. He began reading the book's introductory note. The words and sentences had to be read over and over to get any sense of them. What little he could retain was quickly forgotten. He put the book back on the stool. The concierge stood there, arms folded, watching without expression.

"I don't think I can go right now," Moldenke said. "Maybe in the morning?"

The concierge was displeased but understanding. "Go to your room, then. I hope you have something to show me tomorrow."

"I will, I will. First, I'm going to nap for a few hours, then I'll go over to Saposcat's and have some scrapple. That should generate anger down there overnight. Good afternoon."

Moldenke succeeded in sleeping until dinner time and felt hungry and refreshed when he rolled out of his cot. Downstairs the concierge stood behind her Dutch door. "Good afternoon, Moldenke."

"Hello. I'm off to Saposcat's. I'm sure there'll be something substantial for you in the morning."

"I do hope so." She closed the top of the door.

At Saposcat's, Moldenke pored over the menu, searching for something that would churn his stomach and anger his bowel. It would be good to empty them anyway before bathing in the Old Reactor pool. That would be the last place he would want to suffer an attack.

When the waitress came, Moldenke ordered the scrapple.

"We've got some in the back," she said, then bent over and whispered, "it's a few days old, fair warning. We can scrape off the mold for you."

"I'll have that."

"Okay. Something to drink? What about our special tea? We make it with part heavy water. It's lighter than full heavy."

"That's good. Yes. The tea."

Moldenke enjoyed eating his scrapple, despite the foul taste. It was immediately filling and gaseous and gave him confidence that he would have a movement for the concierge in the morning. The light-heavy tea, clear and salty, slid down his throat like thin syrup.

When he got back to the Tunney, after stopping to piss at the public privy, the concierge was not to be seen. He crept up the stairs to the third floor and down a hall to his room. On the way he passed ten or twelve other rooms. From some he heard sounds: a radio, sobbing, laughing, breaking glass, even the gleeful chirps of a young child. Sometimes at night, he'd heard a man coughing, another vomiting out of a window below. Yet, in the time he'd been here, he'd never seen anyone in the hallways, on the stairs, or in the foyer. There were twenty-four rooms on each of the three floors. If they were mostly occupied, as the concierge had said, where were the other tenants?

Lying in his cot, Moldenke rubbed his ear with the barrel honey the concierge had given him, then fell asleep anticipating his date with Sorrel and a long soak in heavy water.

When he put on his uniform the next morning, he saw that it was rumpled and rank. There was a fullness in his stomach and he was passing gas. A toileting stop downstairs to satisfy the concierge would be first, then a stop at the public bath to get the uniform washed and dried.

"Good morning," he said when he saw the concierge standing at her door looking at him sternly. "Nice day ahead."

"Hurry up. I've been waiting here."

"All right, all right."

Moldenke went to the toileting room with the concierge not three feet behind him, her head inclined toward the ceiling. "Mmmm. I smell it already."

He sat down and picked up the *Treatise*. "It may take a minute, ma'am." He flipped through the pages looking for something of interest. When he came to a chapter called "Of Beauty," he read a few lines to himself, but loud enough for the concierge to hear. "There are some parts of the human body that have been observed to hold certain proportions to each other; but before it can be proved that the efficient cause of beauty lies in these, it must be shown, that wherever these are found exact; the person to whom they belong is beautiful..."

"I don't have all day, Moldenke. There are other guests you know."

"It's odd that I never see them."

"They're probably all out when you're in and they probably come in when you're out. I guess that's it."

"I hear them at night."

"They probably come home later than you do."

Moldenke stopped reading, set the book back on the stool, and had a productive bowel movement.

The concierge said, "Let me see it."

He lifted a buttock so that light could get to it. "There."

"Now wipe and get out of here. I'll flush it and clean the bowl."

Moldenke wiped and pulled up his pants. "Thank you, ma'am."

"Don't forget, you replace the paper you use."

"I'll get some at the public."

"I should make you put that in writing." She fetched an envelope from her apron and gave it to him. "Here, a letter came for you."

"Oh, good. News about my house."

Dear Moldenke,

I made a big effort to find that attorney of your aunt's, but he's dead and his office is closed. There's a big black wreath on the door. They tell me he was exploded for embezzling from his elderly clients. Maybe your aunt's money was stolen. I'm at a loss as to what to do. For now, I'm going to take in more jellyhead boarders with mechanical skills. One who knows about electricity, another that maybe can replace all the rotted floor boards. Even then, materials will have to be scrounged, manufactured, stolen, or borrowed.

By my count, there are six bedrooms and three bathrooms. So we could house a couple more artisans if we had to, although only one of the commodes is working. We'd have quite a lineup in the morning with more boarders and after that a holy stink. You know how it is with jellies. I'm going to find that plumber and make him an offer. The cesspool in the yard looks like a little brown lake. It must be dealt with. We need a proper septic system.

That's the way it is for now.

More news as it unfolds.

Ozzie

On his way to the car stop, worried about his house on Esplanade, Moldenke stopped at the public bath. It was early enough that he had time to bathe while his uniform was boiled and dried and he would still be at Big Ernie's by eight-thirty. The bath aide on duty met him at the door. "I'm sorry, but we're closed today. A bunch of jellies snuck in and drowned themselves in the pools last night. We didn't find them until this morning."

"Are you still washing uniforms?"

"Sure, if you want it stinking like cadaverine. All the pipes are full of bad water."

"I'll just go like this, then. I'm bathing anyway, out at the Old Reactor with my girlfriend." Moldenke raised his head to show the damage to his ear. "We both got deformed."

"Some people tell me the water did them a world of good. Other people say it almost killed them."

Moldenke said, "They were probably too far gone, too sick, too old, too deformed, something like that. At least the cars are running today."

"Some are, some aren't. The ones that are are late."

Moldenke waited at the stop. His guess, going by the sun's height, was that it was about eight o'clock. He looked up and down Arden Boulevard. There was no sign of cars in either direction and the skies were clouding up. The weather could change at any minute and spoil his outing with Sorrel. Or the car could be so late that she would tire of waiting and go without him.

About fifteen minutes later he saw a car going in the other direction, which meant that it would soon be getting to the end of the line and turning around for the ride to the Quarter and out to Old Reactor Road. He would be tardy, but only by an hour or so. Surely Sorrel would know the cars were running late and take that into consideration.

When he climbed into the car, he asked the conductor the time and was answered with a shrug and a dirty look. "You know free men shouldn't carry watches or look at clocks."

"Sorry. I forgot. It's not surprising the cars are so late all the time. I understand now."

A rudimentary gel sack has been taken from a free woman of the city. Previous thinking was that such an occurrence would be impossible. The small, dry, shriveled sack was found in the woman's breast, where it had finally cocooned itself. There had been swelling and pain, which she thought was probably rheumatism, but her entire constitution became so affected that her hands fisted in a way that made them useless, and her face had tanned like a piece of hide. She said that she had been living among jellyheads in proximity of the Old Reactor and that the sack may have entered her system then.

Until the sack was removed, the woman was able to feel it passing from one part of her body to another. She attributed the chills and fever she felt to this action of the sack, which has now been put into a brine solution for observation. In a few days the woman was well enough to travel and did so, saying she was off to the Old Reactor area to rejoin her adopted jellyhead family.

Moldenke's ride to the Quarter was an uneventful one. Being a Sunday, there was no pretend-guard on duty at the Quarter's entrance and the car passed through without slowing down, saving some time. It wasn't enough, though. When Moldenke got off at the stop near Big Ernie's, he found a note Sorrel had tacked to the bakery's door: *Tired of waiting. Meet you there.*

He ran toward the car he'd just stepped from, now on its way to the turn at Old Reactor Road. After chasing it a block, his knees ached, his ear throbbed, and he was exhausted. He stopped, returned to the stop at a leisurely pace and waited. The sun, when it peeked through passing clouds, was three-quarters toward mid-heaven. It was about ten thirty, Moldenke guessed. By the time the car made its rounds and picked him up again it was about noon.

The pond could be seen shimmering beside the concrete dome of the Old reactor as the car slowed for its final stop on the route. There were bathers lounging on the green grass at the water's edge, free children playing, two or three skiffs on the pond. The bathers all wore red rubber swimsuits.

Moldenke saw a free woman, also in a red suit, frying mud fish in a pan over a small fire made of rags, pine cones, and a pair of old canvas shoes. He asked her where to get a bathing suit and she directed him to a rental and dressing area on the other side of the pond.

He lit a Julep and walked along the shore looking for Sorrel and heading for the dressing area at the same time. The weather was holding on pleasantly, the air busy with bees and dragonflies and little biting gnats. Frogs croaked in the mudflats. There were free men fishing in the deeper water. One of them pulled in a big mud fish so heavy it snapped the line and nearly hit Moldenke in the head as it flew. One of the fisherman said, "They're twice as big as what you get at Saposcat's." Another said, "They taste a lot better, too. There's something in the water."

Moldenke asked if any of them knew Sorrel. One said, "Big Ernie's girl?"

"Yes, I'm supposed to meet her here."

Moldenke heard Sorrel's voice. "Moldenke! Over here! In the water!" He spotted her out near the middle, floating on her back. She wasn't wearing a veil and from that distance didn't appear deformed at all. "Oh, that ear," she shouted. "Hurry, go rent a suit and jump in. It'll be much better right away. Look at me."

"I'm sorry for being late. The cars weren't running on time."

"It doesn't matter. Rent a suit and get in."

Moldenke went around to the rental shed and showed his pass card. "Give me a suit, please."

"Size?"

"I'd say medium."

"Everyone seems to be medium these days. All we got is large. People used to be large before the liberation. I'll rent it to you, but it might fall off."

"If that's all you have…I'll hold on to it if I have to."

"Good enough. Here you are. It's been boiled, don't worry. Pick any empty stall to change. Here's your key."

There was a temporary metal structure that looked like a small barn with stalls for changing and hooks for hanging clothes. Moldenke put on the large red suit and hung his dirty uniform to air out. The key turned smoothly in a small padlock that seemed easy to break open using the simplest of tools or a strong pair of hands with a hammer and spike. While he thought it was a pointless act, Moldenke locked the door and put the key in his bathing suit pocket. His uniform had no real value, but he didn't want to go all the way back to the Tunney naked.

He pulled in the bathing suit's sash and cinched it as tightly as he could in his fist then stepped through the cloth curtain into the scene outside. Those who saw him in the over-sized suit were amused. Some of them snickered. One said, "Get in the water. It's heavy. It'll fix that ear."

Moldenke rounded the pond from a different direction. About midway, he spotted Sorrel. She was no longer on her back, but face down in the water, probably trying to give her damaged places a good dosing. He waded into the shallows, worried that when the water was deep enough he would have to let go of the suit's waist in order to swim out to her. Even as the water rose to his knees, he could feel its weight against him. He dove forward and swam toward Sorrel. The buoyancy of the heavy water made it almost effortless. The red suit slid down and off him as he thought it might, floating off among green lily pads out of his reach.

The water supported his light weight even when he stood upright and did nothing. Now he walked in it and paddled with his hands with the sensation that it was closing around his body like syrup or a gel. He dipped his ear in as he swam. When he reached Sorrel, he took one of her feet in his hand. It was a foot that felt good to him. He had never held a woman's foot in his hand.

One of the fishermen called out, "Hey, you, turn her over. She might drown."

Her face was still submerged. No part of her moved. Moldenke placed his hands on her hip and turned her over. She rolled like a log and expelled a long-held breath of air with a mouthful of heavy water. "Oh, Moldenke. Isn't this the cat's meow, this water? Look at my face. I don't need a veil. You should soak your ear more. You should bathe here every day."

Moldenke cupped his hands, filled them with water, and dipped his ear. "You do look very good, Sorrel. *There's* a pretty face on the mend if I ever saw one. You can throw the veil away."

"I'll never be beautiful, so I suppose I'll aim for sublime. Have you read The *Treatise*?"

"A paragraph or two."

"It's funny. When the beautiful are deformed they enter a state of being that Burke claims either equals or tops beauty—the sublime."

Moldenke raised his head, and with his bulbous ear dripping water, slid his hand under Sorrel's red suit, placed it on her cool breast and asked, "Would you consider mating with me?"

"Maybe. I'll ask my father. He'll probably want to have a talk with you."

"All right."

"Let's get out of the water. I'm beginning to pucker," Sorrel said.

"That's fine, but I lost my suit. They gave me a big one and it fell off. It's out there in the lily pads. Let me get it. The key is in the pocket."

"I'll meet you at the rental shed."

"Yes, in a minute or two."

Sorrel and Moldenke walked and paddled through the water in opposite directions.

Brainerd Franklin admitted a reporter on to the grounds of his estate, located on a bluff above the beach at Point Blast. His face was thicker now, the reporter recalled. She hadn't seen him since his heart attack. His hair was grayer. His eyes weren't as bright as they once were, but still pierced. His recurring phlebitis forced him to move slowly, the old self-assured stride replaced by an irritating limp.

He gingerly eased himself into a gray velvet recliner, resting his leg on a matching footstool. "I bought this chair when I was at my peak," he said. "It's been my favorite ever since I said goodbye to the game I loved. My resignation speech was written in this chair, with a glass of bitters right there on that table."

The former exhibition golfer says he did the best he could with the talent he had. "I never thought about being loved. I wanted to golf, that's all. I've married to keep up appearances, but it's cold and distant."

His resignation from the lucrative exhibition circuit has eaten away at his transplanted heart. His sad eyes glanced at a showcase where mementos of his headline-making world tours were proudly displayed. Then he gave a faint grin. "You know, in times like these, you find out who your friends are."

It's no secret that in the aftermath of his retirement many of Franklin's personal contacts abandoned him.

"Come on," he said, limping to the door. "Let me show you around."

The reporter followed him from his rosewood-paneled office and climbed into a yellow golf cart with the name Franklin painted above the grille. As they drove through the estate grounds, taking things at a slow clip, Franklin lamented the sorry state of his former golfing empire. "Those buildings over there were filled with my working staff. Now they've been stripped of furniture. But I'm told that's the way it is for a jellyhead, the ups and the downs. I've had the ups. Now I'm going down." The cart then returned to the main house. "I get out here," he said.

Off to the side, Mrs. Franklin, a free woman, wearing a bright yellow and white pantsuit, stopped puttering in her garden and trotted toward the reporter. "Isn't this a beautiful garden?" she asked. "I just love working with my flowers. That's how I spend most of my time."

When she had gone back to her garden, Franklin said, "Even without love, Sophie and I talk a lot about our shattered lives. I get strength from her. She is at peace with herself. She is truly a great lady."

Franklin was met on the patio by a visiting nurse who removed his gray sports coat and made him swallow two or three pills. She then checked his blood pressure and palpated his wide abdomen, causing him to gasp when her thumbs dug into his spleen.

When the procedure was over, a pained Franklin beckoned to the reporter. "Come see my office. I'll give you a souvenir."

The reporter followed eagerly and stood at Franklin's desk, watching him rummage in the drawers until coming up with an autographed ball. "Perhaps you'll like this. It's the only one I have left. The rest have been sold."

His handshake was firmas she accepted the ball and left.

Moldenke retrieved his red suit, climbed back into it, and went to the changing nooks. The flimsy lock, as he feared, had been broken open. His dirty uniform hung there still, but his pass card was missing from the pocket.

The attendant at the rental shed showed a hardened attitude at first. "Anybody stupid enough to leave it in there with that little lock, I got no sympathy for."

"How will I get on a streetcar?"

"I don't care. I'm about to close."

"Have you seen Sorrel? She must have come here to turn in her suit and change."

"Big Ernie's girl?"

"That's her."

"Ernie came and got her in his motor."

"Did she mention she was *with* someone? This was a date. We were together. I thought she would wait."

"Brought back her suit, changed clothes, and left. That's it."

"All right. Thanks."

"Wait a minute," the attendant said. "I'm feeling bad about this. Look, people lose their pass cards here all the time." He reached into a box filled with them. "Here, take this one." He handed a card to Moldenke embossed with the name Enfield Peters.

"I know him," Moldenke said. "The actor."

The attendant chuckled. "Free people don't need a name. Half the folks in Altobello go around with somebody else's card. Nobody cares. You want another card? I got plenty of unknowns."

Moldenke thought of taking another one but reconsidered when he realized that Peters' name on the card could pave the way for little courtesies and attentions he wouldn't get otherwise. "No, I'll keep this one."

The Peters pass card proved effective when Moldenke boarded the car back to the Tunney Arms. The conductor tipped his cap and smiled. "Evening, Mr. Peters."

"I'm going all the way to the Tunney Arms on the west side."

"Yessir. Sit anywhere you like. I loved you in *Who Puked?* Great film."

"Thank you. It was one of my best."

"It took me a good while to figure out it was the waiter," the conductor said.

"It had to be him. The clues were there all along."

"You don't look like you did on screen with an ear like that."

"They do wonders with powder, wax, and rouge these days, and the lighting, too."

Moldenke took the first seat available, let his head sink down to his chest, and closed his eyes. He wanted to be in a light trance for the long ride back, if not asleep. The clanking of the car's wheels on the steel tracks and the squeal of the rusty springs made any state but hyper-vigilance impossible.

He saw that the passenger sitting next to him was reading the last few pages of the *Treatise* and when his stop came, he got up, closed the *Treatise*, and held it out for Moldenke. "Here, you want this? It's just a load of shit. It'll put you to sleep."

"I'll take it, thank you." The *Treatise* would be just the thing, Moldenke thought, for going to sleep on the car. After reading a few pages dealing with the effects of sympathy in the distresses of others he was drowsy, a few more and he was asleep until awakened by the conductor. "Mr. Peters, you've shit in your uniform. You're getting off here. Do you know where the public bath is?"

Moldenke stirred awake. "I know."

The passenger sitting next to him, with a free child on his knee, held his nose. The child repeated the act.

Moldenke got off at the stop nearest the Tunney and walked down Arden to the public bath. The weather was getting nippy—probably an ice storm on the way. Conditions had been benign for a few days. A change was overdue. He hoped that all the putrid water had been run through the system and that the bath would be open. It was, but with limited services.

"I can wash your uniform and your drawers and your socks, but I can't dry them. The furnace is out of radio gas. And only one pool is open, the first one. The water is nasty. It might be better tomorrow."

"Wash the uniform. I'll wait in the boilery. I have a book."

The bath aide gave Moldenke a towel to cover himself. "I know that book, the *Treatise*. Everybody's reading it. I read it."

Moldenke settled on a bench, lit a Julep, and read Part One, in which Burke claims that terror is not only the strongest of the emotions but the source of the sublime. Ideas of pain, he goes on to say, are more powerful and more memorable than ideas of pleasure.

The bath aide stirred Moldenke's boiling clothes with a long wooden paddle. "Have you gotten to the part where he says that pain is what we remember, not pleasure?"

"I did see that. I can't disagree."

"So in the end, he comes down on the side of the sublime."

"So I've heard."

"What about the chapter on Beauty? Did you read that yet?

"A little of it, maybe."

"He says *love* is the *beauty* of *sex*. Animals have sex without love. Jellyheads have sex, but they behead the ones they love most. We've got love, and that's the beauty of it." The aide lifted the wet, hot clothes with his paddle and flung them into a hydraulic press to squeeze them and return the water in a little wooden chute to the boiler. "Okay, your stuff's ready. I would advise you not to waste time getting to your room. It's cold out there. A big front coming through."

It was warm and moist in the boilery, and Moldenke's clothes, while wet, were still warm from the hot water. When he had them all on, and his boots laced, he tipped his cap to the aide and walked north on Arden into a stiff, icy wind. The Tunney was two and a half blocks away. In hopes of keeping his clothes from freezing before he got there, he walked briskly, afraid that if he ran he risked a slip and fall on the sidewalk's sheeting ice. Better to have a frozen uniform than a fractured skull.

The concierge stood in the Tunney doorway with her arms folded, watching pedestrians go by. Some were fortunate enough to have heavy jackets. Others, like Moldenke, weren't, and his wet uniform was beginning to freeze.

When the concierge saw him coming, she opened the entry door. "Come in before you turn blue. Don't let that ear get frostbite. It looks much better, though."

"It must have been the heavy water bath." Moldenke touched the tip of his ear, and even with numb fingers, he felt a change. It was no longer as rough-skinned or as swollen.

The concierge opened her Dutch door. "Come inside. I have a mirror in the bathroom."

A burst of warm air struck Moldenke's face. He glanced into the small apartment's interior, where a pellet stove burned brightly in the parlor, radiating warmth only as far as the Dutch door. The moment he stepped through the door and turned toward the bathroom, his uniform began to thaw. He was leaving wet boot prints.

"I'm getting the floor wet. I'm sorry."

"Hurry, stand in the tub and take off your clothes." He could hang them in the bathroom, she said. They would be dry in the morning. "For tonight, you can wear some things of my husband's." She went to get them.

Moldenke was happy to be out of the icy uniform and boots and in a warm room. He toweled off and looked into the mirror. There was no question, the heavy water was a curative. His ear was much improved. He wrapped himself with the towel when he saw the concierge returning with checkered pajamas, underwear, and a pair of fleece-lined slippers. "Here, these are cozy. Your room will be cold. All the roomers will be cold in their rooms."

Moldenke suspected that these helpful gestures might possibly come with a return request attached.

"Where are *those* roomers? I hear them at all hours—coughing, crying, singing, being sick, tooting kazoos, twanging Jew's harps—but I never see them. It goes against all odds. I should be running into them in the hallways all the time. I should see them in Saposcat's or at the public, but I don't. I wonder why."

"They're probably all tucked away for the night."

"All right. I do appreciate the loan of the pajamas and the slippers."

"Go ahead and put them on. I won't look." She turned toward the doorway.

Moldenke put on the drawers and the pajamas then sat on the edge of the tub to put on the slippers.

"Are you decent? I'm going to turn around."

"I'm dressed."

She turned back. "My husband was a bigger man. They're loose on you."

"That's fine. The warmth's the thing. Why didn't he take these with him?"

"They only gave him a few minutes to pack."

"Indeterminate sentence?"

"Yes, for selling a wormy apple to a blind man. When they decide you've served enough time, they want you out fast. Or they could forget about you and you'd be here forever," she said. "You'll be quiet going up the stairs, won't you? We don't want to wake the others up, do we?"

"We don't. We definitely don't. I'll stop by in the morning to get my uniform and return your husband's nightclothes. Should I plan to move my bowels for you?"

"No. The pipes'll be frozen by morning. It would be a big mess."

"All right then. Good night."

The concierge put a finger to her pursed lips. "*Shhhh.* Quiet now."

During the night, Moldenke experienced what he thought was a mild seizure. It began when he awakened with fever, chills, and a foggy, detached feeling, and ended about an hour later. He remembered nothing of that time but realized when he turned over to go back to sleep, that he had moved his bowels in the pajama bottoms and in his tossing and turnings had smeared it on the top as well. He sat up the rest of the night naked and cold, smoking Juleps

and worrying about what the concierge would say when he
brought the pajamas back. He faced the choice of either
wearing them soiled or folding them and going downstairs
with nothing on but slippers.

Fearing an end to his toilet privileges either way, he decided to fold the soiled pajamas, cover his privates with them,
go down naked, and present them to the concierge and beg
her to forgive him. He would promise to take them to the
boilery as soon as it was back in business again.

Her Dutch door was open, but she wasn't standing behind it at her regular station. He cupped his hand around his
mouth for volume. "Good morning. Are you back there?"
He heard no response. "I've had an accident with the nightclothes. I'm very sorry. As soon as the weather changes, I'll
take them down and have them boiled…Hello?"

He could feel the warm air coming from her apartment
and ventured through the doorway to get his uniform and
boots. He could see the glow of the pellet stove but no sight
or sound of the concierge. After calling out once again and
hearing nothing, he went into the bathroom. The toilet was
dry and there was a note pinned to the wall above it: FRO-
ZEN PIPES. DO NOT USE! He changed into his dry uniform and placed the slippers and the pajamas in the tub.

On his way out, he saw a pair of bare, bruised-looking
feet at the end of a bed in a dim rear bedroom. "Good morning. I didn't mean to wake you." He took a few steps toward
the bedroom. "I got the slippers wet. I'm sorry." When he
reached the doorway he paused a moment and went in, already sensing that the concierge was dead.

He stood beside the body for a while, smoking a Julep,
wondering what to do. He searched through a closet where
her husband's clothes still hung and found a warm wool jacket that fit him perfectly. It would keep him from freezing on

his way to Saposcat's. As for the concierge, she would keep until he had a chance to get some breakfast and consider the possibilities. He turned down the pellet stove to keep the room cool, closed the bedroom door, and left the Tunney.

He had to lean forward at a striking angle to make any headway in the blasts of polar wind and the wild whirls of dry snow kiting down Arden Boulevard and piling up alongside Saposcat's. Even through the iced-over window he could see Sorrel sitting alone in a booth without a veil. Her head was bowed. Still, he could see red welts on her face. She seemed troubled. There was a package on the floor at her feet, and at the end of the booth, a suitcase.

He tapped her on the shoulder. "May I sit with you?"

"I was hoping you would. I saw you coming. I knew your room was around here somewhere."

"The Tunney, a few blocks down."

"Your ear looks much better."

"And your face. It's almost back to the way it was. You even have some color. But what are those pocks, those red spots on your face?"

"It's a miracle, that heavy water, and a curse, too." She nervously moved the package from one side of her feet to the other. "I want to apologize for leaving you at the Old Reactor pond."

"I took the streetcar. I got home."

"My father wouldn't wait, not for a minute. He was so impatient. Now he's dead and the bakery's closed. I don't know what to do. He was making claws and he sat on the floor and he said he was tired and a minute later he was gone."

"I'm sorry to hear that."

"He made a lot of claws in his time, thousands of dozens. Not too many can match that claim. He was generous with them, too. He gave hundreds away at public events."

"I saw him doing that once. You may remember."

She lifted her package to the tabletop. "This is him, his ashes. I had to send the body all the way to Bunkerville Charnel to get it done. They came back today in a nice little jar."

"A memento," Moldenke said. "A reminder. The flesh has commitments, they say."

"What will I do? I'm afraid they'll send me back to Bunkerville. I came with my father. I wasn't sent here. They'll make me go back. I grew up with all this freedom."

"It would be a shock, wouldn't it?" Moldenke ordered the breakfast kerd with a cup of tea.

Sorrel favored meal and green soda. "I'm determined to stay here. I'll get a room somewhere."

Moldenke saw his opportunity and reacted accordingly. "What about the Tunney? It turns out the concierge passed away and left me in charge of the place. I've got rooms available, too. They're drafty and there's only one flushing commode in the whole place. That one's in my apartment. I'll let you use it whenever the pipes thaw. The tub is off bounds, though. It doesn't drain."

"That's very convenient. Thank you for offering. Running a rooming house, that's a lot of responsibility isn't it? All those tenants with their problems and complaints."

"Actually there aren't that many. I never see them anyway. They're no trouble at all."

"That's odd. I stopped to check on rooms at the Heeney and the concierge said they were full. People were sleeping on the stairs and in the hallways."

"Did you see them? Did you look in and see them, all these sleeping people?"

"I didn't. I took her word."

"These concierges are in cahoots. The fewer occupied rooms, the less work for them. They lie about occupancy.

Give me a couple of hours to get a room ready for you, then come by and we'll move you in."

"That's a relief to me, Moldenke. I'll wait here, drink tea, and read. I brought my copy of the *Treatise*."

"See you after a while, then."

Moldenke needed the time not only to prepare a room but to do something with the concierge's body. It wouldn't be in good taste to invite Sorrel into his apartment with a corpse in plain view. She would raise questions and time would be wasted.

He began the process by going into the Tunney's basement, where he'd never been, to see if it might be a good place to store the concierge until a better solution came along. Who would complain if he took over her duties and her apartment? The husband was gone, she was dead. No one would notice. Later, when he had time to kill, he would probably dig a hole in the basement floor and give her a decent burial. Meanwhile, he'd carry her down and lay her on a blanket. For now, getting Sorrel moved in was his chief concern.

He went down a long stairway into a brick-lined tunnel about twenty feet below the first floor and walked thirty or forty feet further through the tunnel until he came to a large, arch-roofed chamber with small, dingy ground-level windows letting in a faint light. A sign on the wall, stenciled in red, said: *Shelter Capacity 100*. It wasn't clear to him what that meant, but the room was deep and cool, the perfect place to store a body.

He went back up the stairs to get her and found a line of grumbling men waiting at the Dutch door. One of them shouted to him, "Hey, who the hell's in charge here? You?"

"Yes, that's me." He stood behind the door. The men smelled of pine tar and wood smoke. "We need rooms. The goddamn Heeney's burning down."

Another said, "There's going to be a lot of dead."

Moldenke ran to the door and out onto the sidewalk. Over the roofs of other rooming houses he could see the Heeney in full flame, the main beam beginning to sag, promising to soon collapse. White smoke billowed into the cold sky. People ran this way and that. Screams could be faintly heard. A free woman rushing by stopped to catch her breath long enough to say, "A girl set her father on fire. He ran burning through the hallway, down the stairs, spread flames everywhere. It's terrible."

To Moldenke it could be none other than Salmonella and Udo. "I think I know them," Moldenke said. "His daughter must have escaped from the Home. It's a shame there's no one to put the fire out."

"Ah," the woman said, "where would they get the water, anyway? Everything's frozen." She buttoned her collar and headed north into the wind.

Moldenke didn't see that anything would be gained by going to watch the Heeney burn. There were men inside the Tunney waiting for a room, and a body to be taken care of. Sorrel would be there soon. He hoped she would dawdle awhile and watch the fire.

First, he would have the men register, then check their pass cards and give them room keys. He stood behind the Dutch door. "All right. There are four of you. Let me see those cards and you can have a room." The men showed him their cards.

"You the new concierge? Used to be an old woman."

"She went back to Bunkerville. I'm in charge now. I should tell you right away, there's no toileting facilities here and the rooms can be as cold and as hot as hell."

One of the men could see the concierge's toilet from where he stood. "What's that in there?"

"It belonged to the old woman. Her husband installed it. It doesn't work anymore."

"You better not be lying, you dipshit."

"We'll all be using the public one down the street. Here are your keys. You can go up to your rooms. Be thankful you weren't burned alive."

The men climbed the stairs, grumbling and cursing. When Moldenke heard the fourth door close, feeling sure the men had all gone into their rooms, he went to the concierge's bedroom to get her and stood at the foot of the bed, planning to lift her feet, swing her around, and ease her down to the floor. That accomplished, he wondered what the simplest way to get her to the basement would be. The best, he thought, was to drag her. As long as no one saw him doing it, there would be no problem. For padding he strapped a small pillow to her head with one of her husband's neck ties. He didn't want it banging against the stairs.

He dragged her out of the apartment, past the Dutch door, and toward the stairs to the basement. All seemed to be going as planned, until the pillow slid off and her head *thunked* hard the last few steps. He left her in the domed brick room after arranging her stiffened arms as close to repose on the belly as he could accomplish. She looked a bit serene and saintly, Moldenke thought, particularly in the dim light.

When he huffed back up the stairs, there Sorrel stood at the Dutch door, weeping into a handkerchief. "They were lying out on the sidewalk, the ones who were burned. It was an awful thing to see. I feel faint."

"You should lie down. Here, come into my apartment. Lie down on the bed."

Moldenke placed her suitcase in the bedroom closet and offered to put Big Ernie somewhere, but she said, "No, I want him," as she fell onto the bed with the ashes clutched to her breast.

"You nap here for a while. I'll get your room ready. Bottom floor or top floor?"

"I don't really care. I'm exhausted. I hurt from head to toe." She closed her eyes. "I'm sick."

Moldenke sat on the edge of the bed and thought for a moment. He glanced down to see where sunlight struck the floor, telling him it was about mid-afternoon. Perhaps Sorrel would sleep here the entire night. It would be a thing to hope for. He wouldn't get her room ready at all. He would sleep beside her tonight in the concierge's bed. Readying a room could wait.

He edged closer to her so that his thigh lightly touched hers. He was going to say, "Let me rub your back. It might relax you," when he realized she was already asleep.

He didn't want to rub her back now and take the chance of waking her, so he went into the bathroom to see if perhaps the pipes had thawed. A melting had begun, but by no means were the pipes flowing.

He returned to the bed and listened to Sorrel's raspy, labored breathing. He didn't want to think she was dying and thought of other things. There might be a radio in the apartment, one that would dial in a weather report. He searched every likely spot and eventually found an old portable in the drawer of a dresser, dusty and unused, the batteries weak. He turned it on nevertheless, and though the signal was intermittent he heard a Bunkerville news roundup reporting that near there a suspicious red cloud dumped an extra-heavy dose of radio powder on the Black Hole Motel, occupied by fifteen people. The motel has since been deserted. Then came a bulletin from Altobello: Radio poisoning warning issued for Old Reactor pond.

The batteries faltered and Moldenke could no longer make sense of the signal. He put the radio back where he'd found it.

The mail arrived. He could hear the postal carrier's heavy footfalls and a tapping on the Dutch door. He waited until the carrier was gone before checking the mail. He didn't want any further questions about why he was running the place.

There was a letter from Ozzie:

> *Dear Moldenke,*
>
> *I went up on charges yesterday for organizing the milk-men and now I'm going to be exploded next Friday, or maybe the next, depending on how they schedule it.*
>
> *I wonder what it feels like. A quick sense of expansion, then nothing. Is that it? What did I do? Organized? Looked out for the poor working stiff? You would have done the same if you were here. It's all a political thing. I was a threat to them as an organizer. They could see the liberation coming. So I get exploded. What's fair?*
>
> *If the liberation doesn't come very soon, this will be my last letter to you. After they explode me, the two jellyhead artisans living in the Esplanade house will be in charge until you come home, which I hope will be very soon.*
>
> *When you get this, I could be dust.*
>
> *Yours,*
> *Dead Ozzie*

Near dusk, after waking from a nap beside Sorrel, Moldenke heard a rapping on the Dutch door. As concierge, it was his duty to receive would-be tenants, especially Heeney survivors. This could be one of them.

The rapper, however, was Salmonella, with singed hair and a scorched blouse. "I want a room." Her canvas bag, too, was scorched.

"Did you set the fire?"

"He was no good. He was trash. So I burned him."

"If you want a room, show me your pass card. I'll give you a key. But here's a warning, there are men up there whose friends perished in the fire. They won't excuse what you did."

"I don't care. I'm freeborn. I'm not afraid of anything. Why are you in charge here?"

"Things happen. The concierge was called back to Bunkerville. I'm watching out for the Tunney while she's gone. We don't have facilities, so you'll have to use public ones."

"Yeah, I know—same as the Heeney."

"A lot of free people died."

"He ran all around till he fell down the stairs and set the carpet on fire. I didn't know he was going to do that. Please let me stay in your room. I'm tired. I won't have trouble sleeping on the floor."

"You *escaped* from the Home, then."

"It's easy. The Sisters drink bitters and get sleepy. I took a can of turpentine from the tool shed at the Home and went to look for Daddy at the Heeney. He was drunk with bitters and half asleep on a torn-up old mattress with a lit Julep in his mouth. I sloshed him with turpentine and the Julep caught him on fire."

"That explains it," Moldenke said.

"I hated him so much. Now I won't ever know who my mother was."

He handed Salmonella a key. "The room hasn't been cleaned. Things have been so busy. I'll be sleeping down here."

"I don't care. I could sleep in a rat's nest."

"Keep an eye out for those men up there. They may want to hurt you."

"Here." Salmonella reached into her bag for an apple, which she handed to Moldenke. "They grow on a tree at the Home." She began her ascent of the stairs and stopped. From that vantage, she saw the apartment bathroom and the commode.

"It's not for tenant use," Moldenke said.

Passing the fingers of one hand through her singed hair, Salmonella continued to the second floor.

Moldenke could now return to Sorrel and hope there would be no more check-ins for a while. He thought she might be a little peckish when she awoke and he went into the apartment kitchen to see what might be there to eat and drink. He had never seen the concierge at Saposcat's and concluded she must have eaten in.

The kitchen was small, but there was a coal-fired brazier for cooking, pots and pans, and a fresh-box that opened to the outside cold. In the box were cans of meat, meal mix, salted mud fish, a quart of green soda, and on a shelf above the fresh-box, a bottle of bitters. There wouldn't be any real need to go to Saposcat's for dinner. He and Sorrel could stay in, have some meat, a couple of mud fish, soda, an apple, possibly a glass or two of bitters, then get some needed rest.

Things were falling into place for Moldenke, at least for the moment. The concierge in the basement shelter remained something to think about now and then. If the weather turned hot, there could be an urgency to take care of her in some way, either bury her or move her elsewhere.

He sat on the edge of the bed. Sorrel was still asleep, still clinging to Big Ernie's ashes, some of which had spilled from the badly sealed container on to the bed sheets. He leaned close to the pillow, planning to give her a little kiss on the cheek, a brotherly kiss, nothing to frighten her. But when his puckered lips neared her flesh, he felt heat. He touched her forehead. She was feverish. He shook her shoulder gently. "Sorrel? You're hot as a stove. You should be drinking something. We have green soda."

She lifted her head, leaving strands of hair on the pillow, then turned to the side and vomited foamy, rosy bile over the edge of the bed.

Moldenke handed her the corner of the quilt to wipe her mouth.

"Sorry, Moldenke. I couldn't help it. I'm *so* sick."

"It's probably a bug. The weather's been cold."

"It's radio poisoning. I bathed in that pond so many times. What about you, Moldenke?"

"Only that once and not for long."

"Let me sleep here. It hurts to move."

"Would you like anything to eat or drink? I have a kitchen. There's meat, there's green soda. Even bitters if you want something stiff."

Sorrel didn't answer. Her head sank back into the pillow and she was asleep in moments.

Moldenke was in a quandary. If Sorrel was suffering radio poisoning, there was nothing he could do other than let her sleep and make her as comfortable as possible. He tucked the blanket around her and put a second pillow under her head.

As Sorrel slept, Moldenke ate a couple of mud fish along with a few gulps of bitters and settled on the idea of doing something about the concierge. It was nearly dark outside, so what little light came into the basement windows would soon be gone altogether. He had three or four Juleps left and a few matches. He searched the apartment, hoping to find a candle. There was a box of waxed-paper matches near the pellet stove, but no candles that he could find.

Now the bitters were making him dizzy. He descended the basement stairs carefully, his ankle throbbing, holding to the rail with one hand and trying to keep a match burning with the other. The matches cast light in a small circle. Anything a few feet away lay in darkness. He almost stepped on a slug before crushing a fat, brown basement cricket underfoot. When the flame reached his finger, he would stop, blow out the stub, and light another. Once down the stairs, the footing was paved with rounded stones that were damp, uneven and with a slippery skin of mold. He had to take each step with the skill of a mountain goat. A sprained or broken ankle could lay him up for weeks or months.

On reaching the shelter area, he had two matches left, which lighted his way to the body. He stood beside it, regretting he'd come all this way without a thought-through plan for disposing of it in a sanitary way. Several options occurred to him. One, to leave her where she was, do nothing, and hope she would shrivel and dry, though in such a damp environment that was unlikely. She was sure to mold, perhaps even liquefy after a while. In the meantime, there would be cadaverous odors wafting up. The roomers would complain.

The other possibility, dragging her up the stairs and out of the building and who knew how far, would be quite strenuous. He wasn't feeling all that well, and if he were to exhaust himself, he could easily lapse into something far more serious. He made the decision to leave her there. If he detected any odor, the plan would be reconsidered. Until then, it was best to go back to his duties as concierge, to taking care of Sorrel, and to dealing with whatever trouble Salmonella might bring.

He sat in a chair near the bed and kept an eye on Sorrel. She shivered, moving her head from side to side in an agitated delirium. Her face, flush with radio poison, looked radiant and beautiful to Moldenke at that moment. He added pellets to the stove at about midnight, then took off his uniform and lay next to her, thinking that his warmth, however slight, would provide her some comfort.

"Sorrel, can you hear me? Can you understand what I'm saying?" She seemed not to hear him and didn't respond. Strands of her hair had come off and were strewn on the pillow. He saw that her eyes were open. "Can you see me?"

There was again no response of any kind, which convinced Moldenke that if he was ever to mate with Sorrel, this would be the best opportunity. He first removed his socks and underdrawers in a careful way, hoping not to disturb her. He brushed her hair from the pillow with the side of his hand and kissed her lightly on a fevered cheek. Next he unbuttoned her blouse and felt her breasts with the tips of his fingers, encircling the nipples with a gentle sweep. She showed no signs of displeasure or annoyance, so he went further and removed the rest of her clothing. This was not without difficulty. Having to raise much of the weight of her body to slide her skirt and underdrawers off, the muscles in his arms began to twitch and spasm and pain him. He was exhausted when the task was over and lay back to recover his breath. Now the two lay naked together under the cover, dusted with Big Ernie's ashes, she shaking with chills, he fondling himself in preparation for mounting her.

When he felt himself fully aroused, he placed two fingers at the entrance to her *vagine* and pressed them inward, causing her to stir uncomfortably, yet to open her legs wider. He felt that her body, if not her mind, was willing. It wouldn't be a beautiful act, it would be sublime. He let a finger enter the *vagine* and inch or two, then slid it outward and upward. He did this again and again until her hips rose and she presented herself to him. But now he was soft. He fondled himself once more to no effect and in a few minutes gave in to sleep.

At about three, he felt chilled, threw back the cover and sat on the edge of the bed, intending to feed more pellets to the stove. Before getting up he felt Sorrel's forehead, to see if her fever had gotten worse. At first touch, his hand drew back. Her face was as cold as a statue's. She was dead and already a little stiff.

The first Saposcat's, an elegant old restaurant damaged during the liberation, had its re-opening in the Quarter spoiled by a head drop on the part of an organized band of jellyheads. Those dining there were being treated to cuisine prepared in the French style, and this included freshly baked hardcrust bread from brick ovens. The diners were urged also to try the tortoise soup, the tongue salads. Other specialties included meat divan, mud fish *en papillot*. And the best part was the price. With a proper pass card, and for those being released back to Bunkerville, the meal cost nothing.

Along with the serving of soup on opening night came a commotion at the back entrance. Three male jellies walked in with dripping suitcases and cans of deformant. One of them took the lead and tried to calm the full tables. "Look, remain still. Don't vocalize. We have some heads. We will leave them and go. Continue eating, please."

The suitcases were set down near the *maître d*'s station and the jellyheads backed out waving deformant cans. When they were gone, one of the kitchen staff came out in his apron and assured the quivering diners that all was well. "We're very lucky no one was harmed. Keep enjoying your meal. This mess will be remedied."

A little troupe of kitchen help took the suitcases away and cleaned up the leakage with hand cloths and turpentine. After that, despite the bite of turpentine in the air, the diners went on and finished all the courses, including a desert of fluffy lemon soufflés with butterflies and barrel honey on toast.

Salmonella woke up that morning hungry and with a full bladder. She went downstairs and knocked on the Dutch door. "Moldenke, are you in there? Can I use the pot? It's raining outside."

Moldenke opened the top section of the door. "Go ahead, use it." He opened the bottom and let her in.

On the way to the commode she said, "Let's go eat. I'm starving and I want to talk to you about a very serious thing."

"All right."

Salmonella tried to read a snippet or two of the *Treatise* as she emptied her bladder. Moldenke could hear her through the not-quite-closed door.

"What is all this stupid stuff? I don't read that good, you know. I'm freeborn."

"Just something to think about while you toilet," he said, "not to be taken seriously. It's a lot of blather about the sublime and the beautiful."

"What's that?"

"He thinks that beautiful things are things that pose no threat to us, like statues, poems, symphonies, and paintings. The sublime is like things we marvel at, but fear, like all the majestic mountains we've heard about, the storms at sea, the mystery of the night sky—that's what's sublime."

"Who cares?"

Moldenke admitted he didn't care at all. He waited at the door for Salmonella to finish her toileting.

She flushed and stood to see if it all had gone down. The yellowed water swirled slowly around the bowl.

"This isn't working very good, is it?"

"The pipes are half frozen."

On the way to Saposcat's, Moldenke and Salmonella passed the smoking ruins of the Heeney. He regretted even turning his head that way and looking. Among the fallen timbers were burned corpses, some sitting in metal chairs, a sight that set off a twitching in Moldenke's bowels. Salmonella took little notice of the horrible scene, of the stink in the air, or the weeping families waiting for the mounds of smoking debris to cool.

At Saposcat's, the first thing Salmonella said was, "When I was going up the steps last night, I saw somebody sleeping in that bed, in that little apartment you have. Is it your deformed friend from the bakery? What was her name?"

"Sorrel. She's dead, I'm sad to say, of radio poisoning. She passed on last night. Swam too much in the Reactor pond. I'll have to do *something* with her. But my joints ache, my legs are getting weak, if I bend over I get dizzy. It's hard enough to move my own body, much less another. Can you help me out?"

"Things happen," Salmonella said. "I'll help you with the body if you want. I'm strong. I can do things you can't. You want me to dig a hole? Where? In the Park?"

"That would be very nice of you. I'm thinking, though, that there's a cellar, or an old shelter, in the basement to put her. As long as cool weather holds, we're fine. When it thaws, when the ground is good and soft, we'll find an empty lot and get them under some dirt. You can dig the hole."

Salmonella opened her menu. "Okay, let's eat then. Oh, look. There's scrapple today. I want that and green soda. You?"

Moldenke ran his finger up and down the menu, squinting to see the small print. "I can't afford to anger my bowel any more than it is, but I love their scrapple. I'm going to have the scrapple, too, and some tea."

The waitress came and their orders were placed.

"I should tell you," Moldenke said, "as long as you're going to help me with Sorrel, that the concierge didn't go back to Bunkerville. She's in the basement, too. Died all of a sudden. I assumed it would be best if I just took over her responsibilities. Who would care?"

Salmonella folded her arms and pouted. "I think now I'm afraid of those men up there. And that room is cold. Let me stay in your cozy little apartment with you. Your girlfriend is dead. Why not?"

"All right. You can stay. I'll fix you a place on the floor near the stove. There're blankets in the closet."

"I like you. You're nice."

"Well, I try to accommodate."

"What does that mean?"

"It means being nice."

The waitress brought the breakfasts. "Here's your order." She looked Moldenke in the eye. "You look like you haven't heard. Have you heard?"

"I haven't heard anything," Moldenke said.

"They liberated Bunkerville. It happened last night. They just said it on the radio. We'll all be sent back now. That's what the radio says. They're thinking the freeborn might have to stay. Nobody's sure."

Salmonella was perplexed. Her eyebrows arched and she stuck out her tongue and made a hissing sound.

"She was freeborn," Moldenke said. "Doesn't understand what liberation is. Maybe that's why they want them to stay."

The waitress tapped a pencil against the side of her head. "I don't think I do either, tell you the truth."

Salmonella had a bite of scrapple. "I'm not staying."

"Like I said," the waitress said, "it was only the radio. It probably isn't true. You can probably go if you want to."

Moldenke had a bite of his scrapple, hot enough to burn his tongue. He spit it out to let it cool.

"Will they send you back?" Salmonella asked.

"I don't know. How would I know?"

"If they do, I'm going with you. You can't leave me here."

When Moldenke's scrapple had cooled, he ate it hungrily. "I'll probably regret this later."

"Did you hear me? I said I was going with you."

"It's probably a false alarm. Somebody started a rumor. I'm not going to get excited."

Patrons were getting up and leaving in haste.

Salmonella pointed her fork at Moldenke. "Look at them. We should go."

Moldenke polished off the last of his scrapple and stood up. "We have to get back to the Tunney and take care of those two...the things we discussed."

Salmonella smiled, showing teeth greened by the soda. "I'm ready."

They returned to the Tunney to find several of the roomers walking out with their few things. "Hell, man. We're going back to Bunkerville. What about you? There's a big boat leaving from the Point Blast wharf tonight."

"I haven't gotten any official kind of notice," Moldenke said. "I have responsibilities here."

"There's no notice. You just go. We're getting rotated. Don't you get it? The radio is saying it's time to head for the Point."

The men rushed toward the car stop reaching for their pass cards.

Salmonella held Moldenke's hand. "I'm going with you. Let's go. Let's go now."

Moldenke worried. "We can't leave the bodies."

Salmonella shrugged. "Why? We need to get to the Point. What if we miss the boat?"

"Where is Udo's motor?"

"It must be parked near the Heeney. We can find it. I know where he hides the key. We don't have to worry about the bodies."

Moldenke thought it over for a moment. "It does seem nicer where they are than anywhere else we could put them, doesn't it?"

"It's a beautiful place," Salmonella said. "Let's go." She tugged on Moldenke's finger. "Come on, we're going to Bunkerville. Me and you. We'll get along good."

"I have nothing to pack," he said. "These are my only clothes."

"All I own is in this bag," Salmonella said. "We have to find the motor." She led Moldenke out of the Tunney and past the ruins of the Heeney. By then the site was abandoned, the embers out and the bodies taken away by family or friends, or those willing to help out of boredom.

Around the corner from the Heeney, Udo's motor was parked under a flickering street lamp, its roof coated with ash from the fire.

"There it is," Salmonella said excitedly. "The key is hidden in the well of the fifth wheel."

Moldenke sank into a funk. He was leaving behind a nice apartment with a commode and a kitchen. He was leaving behind the lofty feeling of being a concierge with the run of a two-story rooming house. And what would he find when he returned to the House on Esplanade? A shambles? With jellyheads living there?"

The golfer, Brainerd Franklin, has died. A lover of the practical joke, he had asked to be buried in a lace nightgown, seated comfortably in a reclining chair, with an album of Misti Gaynor photos in his lap. "Tell them to hire a backhoe if they must," he said to his nurse shortly before passing on, "move mud, get me in deep. Leave air space within so that beetles and worms have free passage."

The nurse, who says she knew the end was near, told reporters that in his last weeks Franklin had been spitting up whatever he swallowed. His house gown was a sour mess and he had bouts of quivering and loose bowels. He appeared discombobulated, petty and annoyed, clumsy and skittish. In a fit of self-mutilation, he scissored off both ear valves and ate them.

The nurse said she knew the end was near when he took to his bed and refused all food and drink for five days. She remained beside him in the final moments. His last words, she recalls, were "Tell them I'll be back for supper." After uttering them, there was a groan, a gasp for breath, and the great golfer was gone.

When the cortege arrived at the jellyhead cemetery, the excavation was ready, rimmed with green velvet and artificial grass, seeming to invite Franklin's body, which could be seen atop a motor that streamed black bunting from the rear. There were hundreds in attendance, free people and jellyheads alike.

———

Udo's motor had been parked for weeks. Moldenke feared it wouldn't start. He checked the level of heavy water in the tank and located the key in a small magnetic box hidden under the well of the fifth wheel. Salmonella rushed in when he unlocked the front door. There were spider webs in all the ceiling and door-frame corners and mice rustling in a kitchen drawer. Salmonella struck a match, lit a lantern, and the cockroaches scattered.

Moldenke sat in the driver's seat, set the finder for Point Blast, and goosed the starter. The first several attempts failed to warm the water enough to send it flowing through the system. Until that happened, the motor could not be driven.

"It isn't going to start," Moldenke said.

"Pump that little red rod in and out a few times. That's what my father used to do. He told me it was the hot rod."

Moldenke located the red-handled rod and engaged it over and over until it was warm to the touch without success. "I'm about to give up," he said.

Salmonella stomped her foot on the wooden floor. "Keep trying. It takes a while."

Moldenke did keep trying and in a few minutes he could hear water gushing through the main tube.

"Goody, goody," Salmonella cheered. "I'm going to dust out my nook and go to sleep. Wake me when we get to the Point."

"All right."

Moldenke geared up the motor and drove down Arden Boulevard, mostly past darkened buildings. Even Saposcat's and the public privy were closed. Almost everyone had been reprieved and was leaving. Yet when he turned onto Old Reactor Road he could see the lights of the Quarter burning brightly. No one was leaving the gates. They knew that all those empty buildings on the west side would soon fill with new arrivals and customers would return. Now that Bunkerville was liberated, the dispossessed would be coming to Altobello in droves. The older Quarter dwellers had probably seen the cycle repeat more than once in their lifetimes and had come to accept it as the way things went. It was something to be counted on if not understood, like the tides.

A reporter for the *City Moon* had a choice encounter with Mayor Grendon only twenty-four hours ago. The reporter was lunching at a Saposcat's when the perennial candidate came in to eat. It was near freezing outside. A pre-snow sleet crusted the Deli window. The reporter was determined to find a story and intruded at Grendon's table. "Will you make a statement, sir?"

"Of course I will. Stay here and eat with me. The snow is a bluff. In an hour the sun will shine."

The reporter took out her pad and pencil and said she was a journalist.

Grendon said, "Tell them I am long gone but not forgotten. I will run strong come the election. Tell them I have a plan. In the future I see underwater vessels as big as street cars, fish-like in shape, using lateral undulation as propulsion. This form of sub surface transportation will carry thousands at once—Bunkerville to Altobello, Altobello to Bunkerville—with every passenger as happy as a pig. And very inexpensively. Tell them all that."

"A beautiful idea, sir."

"Sublime would be a better word. The sublime always trumps the beautiful."

"What do you see in Bunkerville's future?"

"I can say this: that there will be no more rain. We'll be in a sunspot minimum that will last for twenty years. We will tell the people that grasshoppers store water in their abdomens and that eight or more of them should be eaten every day. It won't be long before we will require one hour of screaming as a daily practice."

Grendon went on to reveal plans to starve himself unless elected. He will be dead by Saturday, the fourteenth day of the fast unless he is elected the day before, in which case he will take food. He'll go this Friday to City Park, rent a pedal boat, and pedal his way to the middle. There he may or may not succumb to starvation, depending on the election results.

"What about housing, sir? Is Bunkerville prepared for the expected jellyhead immigrations?"

"This is what I can say about housing: as jellyheads progressed, they acquired cattle and roamed about searching for pasturage. Then they built a cave of skins to live in. When they learned how to fashion crude bronze tools they began cutting down trees and building homes that resembled log caves. When ice descended from the arctic, driving jellyheads southward where there were no caves, primitive jellies built crude mud huts."

"Thank you so much, sir. Good luck in the election."

"As I've said before, if I'm not elected, my suicide will follow. Ask Zanzetti if he's willing to do the same?"

While Salmonella slept in her nook, Moldenke fought to stay awake. The motor cruised monotonously down the By-way. There were other motors speeding to the Point. Happy riders waved from their windows. "We're going home! We're going home!"

Moldenke felt excited by the prospect of returning to Bunkerville. With his late friend Ozzie exploded and gone from the house, he and Salmonella would assess the situation with the artisanal jellies and see if they could work with them to put the place in order. With attorneys and clerks out of business, the maintenance funds could never be recovered. After the liberation, the currency would be worthless.

Pulling onto Wharf Road at Point Blast, Moldenke saw flood lights moving along the black hull of a freighter, the *Pipistrelle*. Passengers were boarding. He turned back toward Salmonella's nook. "Wake up, girl. We're almost there."

There were dozens of motors arriving, the drivers jockeying for places to abandon them.

Salmonella hurriedly shucked her nightgown and got into traveling clothes.

Moldenke had only begun to look for a good place when the motor ran out of heavy water and rolled to a stop in a cloud of steam.

"It looks like the end of the line," Moldenke said. "Goodbye, Altobello."

Salmonella felt a small touch of sadness at leaving her birthplace.

It was an almost normal Friday night in Bunkerville, two days before the liberation, when radio-poisoned mud fish began to rain down. Anyone outdoors in much of the city was caught in the downpour. Dead fish piled up in gutters and sidewalks quickly. Walking or running was a slippery venture. Pedestrians, in their haste to get out of the shower, stepped on mud fish. Many fell in the process and sustained injuries in addition to a dose of radio poisoning that came with the fish.

There have been other falling-fish events reported from time to time over many decades in Altobello, Bunkerville, and elsewhere. Because the Altobello-Bunkerville fish falls occurred just before the liberation, those prone to superstition thought of them as forewarnings of the momentous changes to come. Many a Bunkervillian shared the belief.

"These fish had to travel from the Old Reactor pond in Altobello," Scientist Zanzetti said. "Something, and we don't know what, sucked them up into the air then carried them hundreds of miles to here. This has been a deadly rain and we expect many will die within months, especially the old and the young."

The affected areas of the city are depopulated and a cleanup is thought to be in progress. Among those poisoned that night was perennial mayoralty candidate, Felix Grendon, who had gone to see Misti Gaynor and Enfield Peters in the comedy hit, *Eventually, Why Not Now?* Hundreds of glowing mud fish fell on him as he emerged from the theater.

With hundreds of returnees on the *Pipistrelle*, there was a shortage of cabin space. Most shivered on deck in the open air. Moldenke and Salmonella considered themselves lucky to find a space to sit down against the fo'c'sle, where they had something to lean back against.

Moldenke closed his eyes for a few minutes of rest, but sat up when his bowel began to anger. There were free people sleeping everywhere. Could he find a place to relieve himself without stepping on them, or worse, cutting loose inside his uniform on the way to the ship's rail? Given that choice, he elected to stay where he was and let go right there if it came to that. He thought back on what he had eaten that day.

"I'm having an attack," he told Salmonella. "That scrapple this morning. It was a mistake. I can't stop it." He lifted a hip and emptied his bowels into the leg of his uniform.

In a moment, the Captain, standing on the fo'c'sle deck, looked over the rail and said to a mate, "Lower a lantern. I want to see what's making that stink."

When the lantern was lowered, Moldenke felt the heat of it on his head. "I'm sorry, sir. It's a condition. These attacks come at the worst times."

"You could have gone to the rail like everyone else."

"I didn't have time to get there."

Salmonella affected a whine. "He's my daddy and he's very sick. Please. Leave him alone."

The Captain turned to the mate. "The returnees are always sick and stinking. I'm going to my cabin and I'm closing the door." He waved to the crowd on the deck. "Good night, all. We'll be in Bunkerville by morning."

In his conclusive study of the jellyhead gel sack, Scientist Zanzetti revealed his findings. These sacks have had a long history of study, always yielding contradictory evidence. The ontogenic contributions of the sack to the jellyhead brain vary greatly. Many theories have been proposed to account for its modifications. Whatever its phylogenetic significance, the gel sack is an important structure formed by invaginations of the head capsule.

When pressed, Zanzetti admits puzzlement. "We can't understand it. The sacks communicate with distant sentient beings or entities, but why? Do they mean us harm?"

An aide of Zanzetti's added, "We think they may be trying to use the jellyheads to weaken or destroy our culture, but haven't perfected the training regimen. That's why jellies do crazy things now. But in the future we see them getting better and better at civil behavior. Their influence then will be so subtle, so insidious, we'll never notice. If this keeps up, we'll *become* them. We'll be jellyheads."

A *City Moon* reporter on the scene asked the famous scientist if he meant that given enough time we could become indistinguishable from jellies.

"If my thinking is right, you can bet on it," Zanzetti said.

"Is there no way to stop it? Is it too late?" the reporter asked.

"Don't worry. Individuals won't feel any change. It will happen slowly, over generations. Every thirty years or so the populace forgets the past. No one's ever the wiser. It's a brilliant strategy. Hats off to whoever designed those sacks."

Salmonella pinched her nostrils closed. "You can't sleep all night with that in your pants, or me either with the smell. Go over to the rail and dump it."

"All right."

Moldenke pulled his pant leg tight to contain the relatively small mass until he could get to the rail, stepping over sleeping passengers all the way.

One of them spat at him. "Watch where you're stepping, you stupid son of a bitch."

Once at the rail he extended his leg over the side and shook out most of the mass. There would be some streaks left behind in his unders and down the leg, but the better part of it was gone. Now he could sleep. He was tired enough that the slight odor that still clung to him wouldn't interfere. He hoped there were still some of his clothes in the closet on Esplanade. He had a disturbing image of going into the house and finding the jellyhead tradesmen wearing them.

Having made his way back to the spot under the fo'c'sle, he fell asleep beside Salmonella, who kissed him lightly on the cheek, then poked him to stop his snoring.

As dawn broke, passengers awakened to a cloudy-but-welcome sunrise and Moldenke wasn't alone in anxious anticipation. As the *Pipistrelle* made her docking maneuvers at Bunkerville Harbor, rumors flew among the passengers as they queued for disembarkation.

"I hear the city is in chaos."

"No law, no money, no property, nothing. Just like Altobello. It's crazy."

"Did they close the hospitals and throw out the doctors? I'm feeling sick. I got radio poisoning."

"A lot of us do. Will they take care of us?"

"You think we'll get pass cards or money?"

Moldenke said, "If they make us wear uniforms, I hope they're nicer ones than these."

There were Bunkervillians out in the streets, gathered into groups, gesturing and talking. Some looked around as if waiting for an indication of what was to come now that the city was liberated, as if waiting for a motorcade with flags, loudspeakers, announcements, and insignias. "Everyone be calm. The city is in good hands." But nothing official appeared. No one knew what to do. Had the liberation been no more than rumor?

Despite the anxiety and confusion on the streets, the Esplanade car from the Harbor to City Park was only an hour or two late. Moldenke and Salmonella ran to catch it. Through the windows they could see that there were only two or three seats unoccupied.

The jellyhead driver turned the crank on his fare meter. "That's a half mil for each."

Moldenke showed his Enfield Peters pass card. The driver cast a quick glance in his direction, then wrinkled his nose and shook his head. "That's no good here, Peters. I don't care who you are. We're still using money until word comes down not to."

"This card is all I have," Moldenke said. "We've been in Altobello."

Salmonella said, "I don't have any money."

The driver shrugged and put the car in gear. "This could all change tomorrow, friend. But till they tell us different, we'll be taking cash. So pay or get off, the both of you."

The passengers began to yell. "Get off! We can't wait all day. You stupid morons."

The car stopped.

"All right," Moldenke said. He took Salmonella by the elbow and led her off.

After walking a few blocks, they passed Bunkerville Charnel, where a jellyhead demonstration was in progress. Forty to fifty of them, faces inked black, stood in front of the building beating on gongs and kettles with dunce caps on their heads. Around their necks were buckets full of stones. The eldest, most enfeebled among them had a deep incision in his neck caused by the heavy weight. They all knelt down on crushed glass, lit candles, looked up at the night sky and repeated the phrase over and over: "Give us liberty or give us death…Give us liberty or give us death."

Scientist Zanzetti floats in the surf off Point Blast, going in and out with the tides. His assistants have spotted him from a distance and thought he was a log rolling in with the cool morning swells. He has rigged himself a tether line more than fifteen miles long, which allows him to float out considerable distances and explore the luminous fauna living near the edge of continental shelf. When he wants to come back to land quickly he need only push a button on his full-body flotation gear and he is reeled in automatically.

The walk from Bunkerville Charnel to the house on Esplanade was thirty or forty blocks. "We'll be there in a few hours," Moldenke told Salmonella.

After they'd walked for an hour, Salmonella said, "I'm hungry. Is there a Saposcat's?"

"In a few blocks."

But when they got there, a sign in the door said, "Relocated to Altobello."

"Oh, no, I'm really starving. I'm growing. I need food and sleep."

"There's a little market at the corner of Broad and Esplanade. If it's open they might accept pass cards."

The market was open, but in the process of closing. Moldenke and Salmonella were allowed in and told to hurry. "We're packing to go," the grocer said, "off to Altobello."

"Strange," Moldenke said, "we were just sent back. It's hard to know what's going on...Do you take pass cards?"

"Yeah, we'll take them. It doesn't matter. We just heard money's worthless now."

"Thanks."

Moldenke and Salmonella walked through aisles of mostly empty shelves looking for anything edible. There were a few tins of meat, some packets of dried mud fish, a bottle of green soda, and a cake of kerd. They gathered all of it into Salmonella's shoulder bag and Moldenke's pockets.

"Thank you, sir. We really do appreciate it. The best of luck in Altobello."

"You live around here? You look familiar."

"Not far. It's a house my aunt left me. I heard there were some jellies living there. I'm a little concerned."

"Don't worry. Those are good jellies, fine jellies. Their cook used to shop in here. They've made that sorry old wreckage of your aunt's into a showplace."

"My old friend Ozzie was living there, too, but he was exploded."

"The hell he was. I just saw him yesterday."

"He was a labor organizer. He violated a law. Didn't they explode him?"

"You're out of touch, my friend. All that stopped when we were liberated. They spared him. He had minutes to go."

It was not welcome news to Moldenke. Dealing with the jellyheads was one thing. Dealing with Ozzie, dull-witted and untrustworthy, was another.

"All right, Salmonella," Moldenke said, "listen to me a minute. When we get there, let me handle the situation."

"Stop worrying."

"All right."

They walked the remaining blocks in the hot late afternoon sun and were standing on the porch of Moldenke's house on Esplanade when Ozzie came around the side with a dripping garden hose.

"Moldenke?"

"I'm back. This is my friend, Salmonella. She's freeborn."

"Hello. I'm Ozzie."

Moldenke chuckled awkwardly. "The place looks grand. I'm surprised. Fresh paint, running water, no broken windows, all the brickwork tuck-pointed. I'm happy to see this."

Salmonella said, "We're hungry. We've got food. Can we go in?"

"Yes, but please be quiet. The jellies are napping. They work hard in the morning and late at night, they nap in the afternoon. I'll go in through the back and meet you in the kitchen."

Salmonella entered the foyer first and paused at the stairs leading to the second story bedrooms. Moldenke followed, past a tall clay pot holding four umbrellas, then the stairs leading to the second story bedrooms and a long low-boy that he recognized as his aunt's. On it was a copy of the *Treatise.*

"What's that...? Listen." Salmonella cupped her ear. "From up there?"

Moldenke listened closely. "It's the jellies snoring."

"What about us? Where do we sleep?"

"I don't know. We'll ask Ozzie."

They went into the dining room. Moldenke recognized his aunt's round oak dining table set with four placemats and her silverware. He could see that two of his friend Myron's typewriter portraits were still hanging in the hallway, clean and free of dust.

Ozzie took off his boots in the mud room and came through the back door. "Let's sit in the kitchen, you two. If you're hungry, one of the new jellies here is a cook and he made some very nice sheep's liver scrapple. It's just about to come out of the oven."

"I love scrapple," Salmonella said. "What's a sheep? I know what a pig is. I know what a cow is."

"A grazing animal. People used to shear them for wool," Moldenke said, "to make warm jackets."

Ozzie removed the scrapple loaf from the oven. "Old man Burnheart down the street keeps a few sheep in his yard. People say he used to be a surgeon. Sometimes he comes down here with a bucket of organ meat. I don't know what he does with the rest of the animal."

"That's very interesting," Moldenke said, "but what I want to know is…how many do we have here now, Ozzie?"

"Jellies?"

"Yes, jellies."

"With the cook and the gardener, that's seven. They're two to a bed now."

"This is my house. You were sleeping in an alleyway. I was desperate to find someone."

Ozzie was insulted, a little angry. "Look at this place. It's far better than when you left it. No rats, no rot, good roof, a place to shit, clean as a whistle. It wasn't me alone who did all that. It was the jellies. They like me. We get along. How about some stew? Want a glass of bitters?" He slid a pack of Juleps from his shirt pocket. "Smoke?"

"Yes. All of that. I haven't had a smoke in weeks. Big shortage in Altobello."

Ozzie poured two glasses of bitters and lit Moldenke's Julep. "Excellent bitters, made right here. The jellies and I brew it in the back yard."

Ozzie sliced the scrapple and fried it in a pan.

Moldenke inhaled the minty Julep smoke and spoke as he held it. "We were told Bunkerville was liberated."

"I don't know. People are leaving. There's a lot of confusion. Right now it's smart to stay home and hope for the best. At least it saved me from getting exploded." He plated slices of scrapple. "There, eat up. The little grocery is closing, you know. Can't say how long we'll be able to get certain things. This is the best we can offer right now."

Moldenke emptied his pockets, laying the items out on the table. "This is the last they had."

Salmonella asked, "You got any green soda?" She had a bite of the scrapple.

Ozzie popped open a soda from the cooler and gave it to her. "We got three left. The ice house closed, so this is the last of the cool ones. Enjoy it."

Salmonella guzzled the green soda between bites of scrapple, grunting with pleasure.

Moldenke wondered aloud if pass cards would eventually be recognized, or would he need money to get by. He wondered, too, if Ozzie thought they'd be wearing uniforms, and if so, where to get them.

"I don't know, Moldenke. I'm staying out of the fracas. I feel lucky to be alive right now. I don't want to show my face out there. Anyway, there are no more real workers to organize. No one works now except jellies."

Moldenke finished his bitters and Ozzie poured a second round.

"Is there a radio? Do you have any news?"

"The station is off the air."

Salmonella wiped her lips with a linen napkin. "That was good. Now I'm tired. Where do we sleep?"

"I'll roust a few jellies and free up a couple of beds. They don't care. They'll sleep in the shed."

"We only need one," Salmonella said.

"Two," Moldenke said. "We'll need two."

Salmonella pouted jokingly.

Zanzetti made news today with the announcement of Molly, a mechanical mother he and his staff are developing. "Free mothers will no longer need to pay the psychic wage of making milk," the scientist says, "because it comes from Molly's breasts in great squirts." The milk, rich in folic acid and lactose, is infused with a mollifying agent to help curb unwanted impulses and instill a modicum of conscience in free-born individuals.

"Those raised in pure freedom, where everything is permitted, never develop a sense of right and wrong. Remorse is unknown to them. Any action is the same as any other action. Can you imagine walking your body around in a world where nothing matters? There would be pandemonium."

If Zanzetti is successful in this pursuit, mother machines in their milk will alleviate those raw necessities of child rearing and allow free women to go about a more productive business, to dabble in cottage industries such as bee culture and candle making without fear of raising unsocialized children.

Ozzie poured another round of bitters. "The sun's still up. It's too early for bed."

Moldenke crushed out his Julep and swallowed down the glass of bitters. "Is it safe to assume you've been in the attic?"

"One of the jellies was up there mixing paint and he found the shoebox. We spent the money fixing the place. You should be happy. Money is either worthless now or will be soon. It was well spent, my friend. We can all live comfortably here as free people."

"It will be too crowded," Moldenke said.

"Not with *these* jellies. They seem to have a very mature philosophy of service. They work hard, they nap, they don't eat much, they stay out of the way, they're easy to live with, and they're always improving the place. Your aunt couldn't ask for anything better."

Salmonella reached into her bag and brought out the sack of apple seeds. "Can I plant these in the yard?"

Ozzie beamed, "Sure you can, girl. I'll have the gardener give you a hand."

Salmonella stood up and clapped. "Oh, goody!"

Moldenke shrugged. "All right. We'll see how it goes."

"You'll meet the jellies later."

Moldenke said, "I've soiled my uniform. Can I take a bath?"

"Of course you can. In your aunt's bathroom, upstairs. We've kept it as it always was. Your uncle's clothes are still in the chiffonier. Wear those."

"That's very thoughtful of you, Ozzie."

Moldenke excused himself and went upstairs to bathe. His aunt's bathroom was adjacent to her bedroom, where he selected one of his late uncle's jumpsuits to wear after the bath. The bedroom was as he remembered it, other than the wall paper, which had been stripped away and the walls painted a mint green. The lamp on her vanity shed light on bottles of fragrance, atomizers, and a pin cushion. Her collection of spoons from all the great cities of the world hung nearby.

At about sundown Ozzie went upstairs and rousted four jellyheads to make two rooms available to Moldenke and Salmonella, who remained in the kitchen eating scrapple.

The jellies came down the stairs yawning, unsteady, holding to the rail. When they shuffled into the brightly lit kitchen, they were almost blinded. Their eyes closed and they leaned against the wall. Ozzie said, "This is Brewster, who gardens; Lester, the mason; Charles, the plumber; and Frank, the painter." The jellies smiled politely and rubbed their eyes. "And our guests are my old labor-organizing friend, Moldenke, and Salmonella, an orphan in his charge, or his companion, or girlfriend. I don't know."

"I'm a girl and I'm his friend," Salmonella said, reaching for a handshake.

The jellies seemed to take pleasure in the act, holding her hand over long, and discharging drops of gel from their ear valves.

The mason said, "Hello. I'm very pleased to meet you. Sorry for the smell. We can't help it. The valves leak."

The gardener said, "Mr. Ozzie tells me you have apple seeds. That makes me very happy. We will start them in the greenhouse then plant the little saplings in the yard. We have a pile of compost out there and quite a bit of sawdust, but it will be years before we have apples."

Salmonella beamed, fingering her sack of seeds. "I'm young enough to wait."

Ozzie said to the jellies, "You'll be sleeping in the shed tonight. Our guests need your rooms."

"Guests?" Moldenke questioned. "This is my house."

Ozzie poured Moldenke another shot of bitters. "Once we're officially liberated, it's just as much mine as it is yours. And these jellies will own it too. So we better learn to cooperate right now and be ready."

"When will it happen?" Moldenke asked. "Is the liberation already underway? How do we know what to do or how to act?"

"It hardly matters," Ozzie said. "We'll do well here either way."

"I'm going to bed," Salmonella said.

Ozzie pointed to the stairs. "It's the first one to the right at the top. I've changed the sheets. They get sticky with gel."

Salmonella said her goodnights and went upstairs.

The four jellies held hands. Ozzie led them out the back door, saying "Good night, my friends." When they had managed the steps down into the yard without falling, he shut and bolted the door. "There's a radio in the shed and some cots. They're perfectly happy to lie down and listen all night to rebroadcasts of Franklin's best-played games. I'm telling you, Moldenke, under the circumstances, we have a good thing here. We're practically self-sufficient."

"I'm going for a walk," Moldenke said. "I need to think about all this. Is the old Come On Inn still open?"

"I don't know. Some taverns are staying open, some have closed."

Moldenke walked a few blocks then caught a streetcar going to Broad Street. "I'm surprised the cars are still running," he said to the conductor when he got on.

"No one's told us to stop."

"Do you take pass cards from Altobello?"

The conductor examined the Enfield Peters card. "I've heard of you, Mr. Peters. Take any seat you want. There's hardly anybody riding the cars tonight. They're all staying home. Nobody knows what's happening."

"I'll get off at the nearest stop to the Come On Inn. Are they open?"

"I've seen the lights on."

The stop was within sight of the Inn. Moldenke saluted the conductor. "Thanks."

"Good night, Mr. Peters."

The Come On Inn was quite the same as it had always been, the air stale, the floor covered with a layer of sawdust, the bite of Julep smoke stinging the nose.

Moldenke sat at the long bar. "What have you got?"

"We got jelly-made bitters. None of the real stuff. Can't get that anymore."

"I'll have a double shot. Do you take pass cards?"

"Till further notice."

Moldenke showed the Peters card. "I'm just back from Altobello."

"You're Enfield Peters?"

"Yes, the actor."

"I saw you in, what's that one? Somebody puked in the sink? They tried to figure out who did it."

"Yeah, I was in that. It was the dishwasher who did it."

"You don't look like you did in the movie."

"I've been deformed. It changed my face."

There were other patrons moving closer to Moldenke, thinking he was the famous actor. They wanted to hear what he had to say. He began to enjoy playing Peters. Letting go of himself, he felt as Peters must have felt—healthy, handsome, tall, imposing. He welcomed the attention and the respect, no matter how shallow.

Then one of the patrons said, "He looks like a guy used to live around here, used to come in here. His name was Molinski or something."

At that moment, a jellyhead carried a five-pound rat by the tail into the Inn. "Anybody want to buy a rat?" the jellyhead asked. When the barkeeper ordered him out, he dangled the rodent near Moldenke and allowed it to sink its teeth into his shoulder. Later, others at the bar said the animal that attacked Moldenke was eighteen inches long from its snout to the tip of its tail.

"Look, it even bites," the jellyhead had said as the animal attacked.

In the commotion that followed, the jellyhead dropped the rat and ran from the bar. Bar patrons killed the big rodent by stepping on it and sticking it with pocketknives.

Moldenke opened his uniform jacket and slid the undershirt off his shoulder. There were teeth marks and beads of blood.

"This guy's not Peters," one of the patrons said.

The bar keeper tore up the card and flung the pieces at Moldenke. "Get out of here you impostering son of a bitch."

Out on the street, Moldenke wondered if there were clinics open, a doctor's office, some place where he might have the rat bite looked at. Even in the best of times, there would be no doctors' offices open this time of night. There was Charity Hospital, run by the Sisters of Comfort, way up on Broad Street. He would have to catch a streetcar. No, that would be too strenuous. And he might find the Hospital's doors closed. The only thing to do was walk back to the house on Esplanade, wash the bite, and hope it would heal cleanly.

Photographers' bulbs flashed as two hundred jellyheads stood in the mud of City Park Wednesday night awaiting a miracle. They watched a nine-year-old jellyhead, Joseph Vitolo, pray at an improvised altar banked with pissweed and dandelion flowers, statuettes and dozens of guttering candles.

It was the sixteenth night the boy had seen a vision of the future in the rain clouds. He later told the press that in the vision he had foreseen a miraculous eddy opening beneath him, swallowing him entirely and admitting him into the ranks of the great saints and healers. The crowd saw no miracle yet, but several invalids and one or two with gel sack rot claimed their condition had suddenly improved.

At seven p.m. the boy rode through the waiting crowd on the shoulders of a neighbor in a hard rain. Paralytics, others with crutches and bandages followed, trying to be near the visionary boy. The parade of soaked jellyheads went along in a semi-circle until the boy grew dizzy and almost fainted.

"Look! Look!" a rumor spread through the lot. "He is not getting wet. The rain doesn't touch him. It *is* a miracle. This is the one who has come to save us."

But those closest to the boy said he was as wet as anyone.

The streetlights along Esplanade were out for the night, but a half moon lit the sidewalk such that Moldenke could step over any holes or wide gaps. When he got to the house, the door was locked and it was dark inside. He went along the porch to the tall window and looked in. A candle burned on a table in the parlor. Now he could see three jellyheads sitting there drinking bitters. He knocked on the glass. All three turned toward the window.

"Can you let me in? I've been bitten by a rat. I need to clean the bite."

One of the jellies came to the window. "Who are you? What do you want? We have nothing to spare. Move on."

"No, I'm Moldenke. This is my house. Ozzie must have told you."

He turned to the others. "Did Ozzie say anything to you about this character?"

"Yeah, let him in."

The jelly went to the door and unlocked it. "Come on in. I'm Jerry, those two are Leon and Jack."

"Yes, Ozzie mentioned you all. I've met four others. How many are here?"

Jerry looked at the others.

Leon said, "Seven, I think. Maybe eight."

Jack said, "We come and go."

"You've done a great job on this place."

"Yeah, we love to work. You want some bitters?"

"I'd like to go into the kitchen and clean this bite on my shoulder first."

Jerry said, "You better. Rat-bite fever's nothing to mess around with. People can die of it. We can't."

Moldenke moved toward the kitchen sink. "It was a big one, too," he said, sliding his shirt down over his shoulder. "The teeth went in deep."

The half-oval bite mark had a rosy ring surrounding it and a purple rash nearby. He turned on the hot water faucet and waited with a kitchen sponge in his hand.

"No hot water anymore," Leon said. "The City turned off the gas today. It's part of the liberation."

Moldenke applied sponges full of cool water to the bite until the dried blood was gone, yet the look of the inflammation frightened him.

"They closed the hospital, too," Jack said. "Pour some bitters on it." He brought the bottle to Moldenke, who wrung the sponge dry and poured bitters into it. Though the application stung him acutely, it gave him confidence that dangerous germs were being killed.

"We got good honey, too, from the Old Reactor. Put some of it on there. It's got radio energy."

Jack said, "One of my sacks had a problem a while ago. The signals were not coming in. That honey took care of it. I'm telling you the truth."

"I have chills," Moldenke said. "I want to go to bed."

"You sure you don't need some honey on that?"

"No, no. I'm all right. Where should I sleep? Where's Ozzie?"

"Maybe he's up there tucking that orphan in."

Fevered now and growing weaker, Moldenke only wanted to find a bed himself. "Where should I sleep?" he asked the jellies, who were sitting at the table again, looking at the candle, entranced.

Leon said, "Your old aunt's room. It's yours now. Go up there."

Moldenke's hands were cold and moist. Almost fainting and nearly collapsing at the top of the stairs, his legs ached terribly and he had no sensation in his feet, forcing him to take small, shuffling steps to his aunt's room, where jelly-heads had been napping.

Without removing his uniform, he fell into the unmade bed, sank his head into a gel-smeared pillow, and pulled the covers up to his eyes.

During the night his fever worsened. When morning came, he awakened to find Salmonella sitting on one side of the bed and the jellyhead gardener on the other.

"Good morning," the jellyhead said. "We need to talk to you about some things."

Moldenke turned his head toward Salmonella. She was smiling. He saw that the blue spots on her teeth had grown even bluer.

"His name is Gus," she said. "He's the gardener. We mated last night so we're together now, me and Gus."

"She'll have my babies," Gus said. "They'll be freeborn."

Salmonella outlined the contours of an apple with her hands. "We're going to grow apples in the back. He promised me we would."

Moldenke said, "Please, I've got rat bite fever. Get me a doctor. Is there a doctor anywhere around?"

Gus said, "There's that old man down the street. Maybe he can help you. I'll go and get him. He lost his doctor's license a long time ago, but he still knows a lot. He was trained under Zanzetti."

"Please, go ask him to come here. I can't possibly get out of this bed. I'm too weak. I'm afraid I'm dying."

"Okay, we'll see if I we get him to look at you."

Salmonella took Gus's hand and the two left together.

Moldenke went in and out of consciousness for the hour it took them to return with a gray-haired man who sat at the vanity and looked at Moldenke from a distance. "I'm Dr. Burnheart, former student of Zanzetti's. Can you see straight? Do you have blurriness?"

"I'm not seeing straight and, yes, things are blurred."

"With a high fever."

"I'm burning."

"And chills?"

"I shiver all the time."

"They tell me a rat bit you."

"A big one."

"Is the bite infected?"

"Yes, and I ache all over."

"Swollen joints?"

Moldenke felt his knee, then his ankle. "Yes."

"Constipation?"

For the first time he could remember, he had no urgency in his bowel. "Yes."

"You certainly do have rat bite fever. It always tightens up the tract. My fear is that it will go to the lining of your heart." The doctor placed a small bottle on a bedside table. "Here are some analgesic tablets. It's all I can do. Nothing else is available with the liberation in place. Have someone get you some water and take three of these twice a day. You need to rest until the fever passes, and we hope without damage to the heart."

"All right," Moldenke said.

"Make him some kind of broth," the doctor said.

Salmonella squeezed one of Moldenke's bare toes. "We'll take care of him," she said, "till he's completely better."

Gus clasped his rough hands in prayer and bowed his head.

"He's praying to Godboy," Salmonella said. "They think he's come to save them."